ACTION WORDS:

JOURNEY OF A JOURNALIST

ORA M. LEWIS

A DESEGREGATION NOVEL

1935 to 1936

Shaune Bordere

Action Words: Journey of a Journalist

This is a work of historic fiction. Though many of the names and characters are factual, it is a product of the author's imagination and the characters, places and incidents are used fictitiously.

ISBN: 978-1-5136-1909-5

FIRST EDITION

Printed in the United States of America

To Ora M. Lewis

CONTENTS

INTRODUCTION

INTRODUCTION

Ora M. Lewis was a phenomenal person. Although *Action Words: Journey of a Journalist* is essentially fictional, her life was remarkable. She began her writing career as a student in high school. Ora sacrificed her prodigious scholastic plans to literally dedicate her life to desegregation. Not only did she lead the desegregation of the City of New Orleans as early as 1938, but she reached the nearly insurmountable feat of desegregating the deeply divided school system. Ora was a journalist, poetess, author, educator, counselor and activist. She was born in 1918 during the First World War. Ora tragically lost her mother in 1925 at the age of seven. She was raised by her grandmother and great grandmother in the New Orleans 7th Ward community. The continuity of their support and love for Ora transformed her life. Ora's strong faith guided her steadily through the Great Depression and the assassination of celebrated Louisiana Governor Huey P. Long. She was inspired to transform a city uncharacteristically affected by Jim Crow traditions. Ora's life was potentially prophetic and it will be remembered for centuries to come.

CHAPTER 1 / "THE COMMITMENT"

Ora Mae Lewis runs to catch Sepia Socialite Editor Alonzo Willis. She's wearing a slightly worn white shirtdress with a thin black belt and white leather sandals. Her long dark hair falls and flies as she stops abruptly. "Alonzo, please. Do you have a moment?" asks Ora. She grabs Alonzo's arm. He towers over Ora and looks down at her frail frame. The small crowd gathered at the podium chatters in a buzz of excitement over Dr. Carter G. Woodson's lecture on segregation.

"Ora, is the matter urgent?" demands Alonzo.

"Aren't you here for Dr. Woodson?" he asks.

"I'm here because of segregation, Alonzo. I'm here because Mayor Walmsley is very dangerous and he poses the greatest threat to desegregation in New Orleans," says Ora.

"I'm not sure of that, Ora. Mayor Walmsley is biased, but he's not the biggest threat," retorts Alonzo.

"Have you read my letter on segregation and Mayor Thomas Semmes Walmsley's Jim Crow attacks?" she inquires.

"Ora, I've read your theory on Huey P. Long's fight with Mayor Walmsley over voting rights and segregation," he replies.

"It's just the beginning, Alonzo. I have so much more in my head. If I could just join the staff, I wouldn't let you down," she begs.

Alonzo grabs Ora by the shoulders and looks her in the eyes. "Ora, you're just not ready for this level of writing. There's too much at stake," demands Alonzo. He pats Ora's shoulders then turns and walks away toward Dr. Woodson.

Ora sulks in despair. She watches as Alonzo and the crowd flocks toward Dr. Woodson.

Alonzo shouts, "Dr. Woodson, Xavier is a nice surprise for a small campus in New Orleans, isn't it?" Dr. Woodson and the crowd all laugh out loud. Alonzo approaches Dr. Woodson and shakes his hand. "Does Huey P. Long have a chance against FDR in light of segregation and the economy?" asks Alonzo.

Ora turns to Alonzo and smiles realizing the intent of his question.

Dr. Woodson responds, "If Louisiana has a chance, then so does Huey P. Long."

Alonzo turns to Ora, smiles and winks. Ora walks over to Alonzo to observe his work.

"Segregation is a system that's designed to control and entrap Black people. We cannot break free without education. Huey P. Long is one of the few who has provided access to adequate schools and books for people of color in the South. He is to be commended," says Dr. Woodson.

"He's creating jobs for us too," says a reporter.

"Jim Crow segregation is deadly in most parts of Louisiana and the South. They attack the Black press and any semblance of organized systems to render us powerless," says Dr. Woodson.

Xavier University's Board Chairman, Clement Stacks, walks over to the podium to address the crowd. "Dr. Woodson, Xavier University and our Board would like to thank you sincerely for your presence here today. Your words are enlightening and thought provoking for our students and our community. We hope for an opportunity for you to return to our small campus again in the near future. Guests and members of the press, we thank you as well for taking part in this event."

The crowd applauds as Dr. Woodson raises his hand in acknowledgment. The crowd begins to disperse as the campus staff gathers chairs and tables. There's an air of bravado in the room.

"It was great to see you today, Dr. Woodson. Have a safe trip back to Washington, D.C.," says Alonzo.

"It's always good to see you again. Stay strong," responds Dr. Woodson.

Alonzo turns toward the hall door when Ora stops him. "Could you give me a ride home, Alonzo?" requests Ora.

Alonzo turns to Ora and says, "Only if you promise not to argue with me about writing. Follow me."

"Of course," responds Ora.

"I'd like you to know where the library is on campus. It's very important that you begin to read and study and think like a writer, Ora," Alonzo says.

"I visit Xavier's library often. It's where I read about Dr. Woodson, Huey P. Long, President Roosevelt and even Mayor Walmsley," says Ora.

Alonzo turns to Ora in surprise. "Why are you so naive about segregation?" he asks.

"I'm not naive at all. I believe that freedom is here for the taking, Alonzo," she says.

"Ora, we're so far away from the end of segregation. You have to wake up. Come on. Let's head home," says Alonzo. He turns to the edge of the campus and walks Ora to his car, a black 1935 Ford Model 48 730 sedan. Alonzo pulls the door handle as he unlocks the car with his keys. He opens the door, then picks up his briefcase from the front seat. He places the briefcase on the floor in the back of his car. "Ora, hop in," he says. Alonzo reaches over to the passenger side of the car and opens the door for Ora.

Ora walks to the passenger side and takes a seat. She closes the door behind her. "Thank you again, Alonzo," says Ora.

Alonzo turns the key to his ignition and drives to

Carrollton Avenue. He stops at the traffic light. "So what's on your mind?" asks Alonzo.

Ora says to Alonzo, "When did you begin to realize that you might be the only voice that Black people in New Orleans might hear that sounds like freedom?"

Alonzo stops and sighs. He rolls his window down, then responds. "When I started the Sepia Socialite I often thought about your dad, Ora. I thought about why he left during the lynchings and I wanted to send a message to Black people and whites that I wasn't too afraid to tell the truth in black and white on paper," he says.

"My dad speaks so highly of you," says Ora.

"Ora, when your dad left, it was like the community was empty all of a sudden. I was scrambling for answers and we were all so disappointed. I never wanted to feel that way again," says Alonzo.

"I live with that reality everyday of my life, Alonzo," says Ora.

"Ora, I understand, but you can't just wake up one day and become a journalist. It takes a lot of hard work and dedication. You must finish school," Alonzo says. He turns right onto Esplanade Avenue.

"Alonzo, I won't ask you again. When you're ready

for me to write, I'm sure you'll let me know," she replies.

"Ora, what's the situation with you and your family? Have you given up on school?" asks Alonzo.

"It's personal, but I think you already know that I'm in need of work. Without my mother, we're always struggling to make ends meet, Alonzo," Ora reveals.

"Ora, you shouldn't have to thrust yourself into the dangerous world of desegregation journalism just to make ends meet," he says. Alonzo turns left onto North Galvez Street toward 1940 Annette Street, Ora's home.

"I could write for the *Times Picayune* newspaper if I really tried, but that's not the type of journalism that I hope for," she replies.

Alonzo parks in front of Ora's home and says, "Well, Ora, I'll give your proposal some thought, but you know how I feel about your education and finishing school."

"I understand, Alonzo. I'll just try to be patient and hope for the best," says Ora.

"Ora, let me get the door for you," says Alonzo as he climbs out of the car and walks over to the passenger side. Alonzo opens Ora's door and she stands on the curb.

"Thank you, Alonzo. This was a really good day for

me, despite the rejection," comments Ora.

"Now hold there one minute. I haven't said no just yet," retorts Alonzo.

"I know you haven't, but you also haven't said yes," she replies.

"Ora, please tell your grandmothers that I found you at Xavier today and that I said hello," Alonzo says.

"Ma Mum and Ma Mere would be glad to see you," she replies.

"Ora, it's been a long day. Let's plan to get together soon when Louise is here with me. How does that sound?" he asks.

"That would be nice, Alonzo. Please tell Louise that I said hello," says Ora.

"I will, Ora. Keep writing those interesting letters and working hard in school," says Alonzo as he returns to the driver's seat of his sedan. Ora waves goodbye. Alonzo starts the car and drives away. She turns to climb the stairs and walks toward the front door.

Ora's grandmother, Josephine Atkinson opens the door as soon as she sees Ora. "Sweetie, what happened today with Alonzo?" asks Josephine.

"Ma Mere, seeing Dr. Carter G. Woodson was

amazing. He spoke so clearly on segregation. I wish that I could write for his Negro History Bulletin," responds Ora.

"But, Ora what happened to the Sepia Socialite? What was Alonzo's response to your interest in a writing position with him?" inquires Josephine. She walks Ora over to the kitchen and offers her some dinner. "Have some fried catfish, Ora," says Josephine.

"Ma Mere, Alonzo just didn't like my letter on Mayor Walmsley's Jim Crow antics. He says I'm not ready to join the staff. He thought that I'd never been to Xavier's library and that I had a lot more reading to do," says Ora.

"That's alright, sweetie. We really need you to begin writing, but they'll be other chances," Josephine says.

"Ma Mere, Alonzo did actually say that he's thinking about it, but he's concerned that I'm not in school," Ora says.

"Ora, Alonzo is one of the few people who knows your circumstances better than most. Hopefully, he'll have a change of heart," says Josephine.

Ora's great-grandmother, Ellis Atkinson enters the kitchen. "Ora, I'm so glad you made it back in time for dinner," she says.

"Good evening, Ma Mum. Alonzo was kind

enough to give me a ride home from Xavier after Dr. Woodson's lecture," Ora says.

"Is there any good news from Alonzo?" Ellis asks.

"Not yet, Ma Mum. He's just not ready to hire me," Ora responds.

"Ora, there's an event tomorrow at City Hall where Mayor Walmsley will speak. I'd like you, Cleo and Alexia to attend the speech and cover the event in your own way. You can really show Alonzo what you're capable of that way," suggests Ellis.

"Ma Mum, I don't know. I really try to avoid Mayor Walmsley as much as I can, because he's so vicious. Remember what he did to Black voters recently? The man's dangerous," Ora says.

"Listen to me. Half the city will be there. The police will be there, and so will the press. Walmsley won't try anything funny tomorrow, Ora. Just trust me," insists Ellis.

"Ora, leave early for the speech and take good mental notes. Write your next letter to Alonzo from experience instead of second hand sources this time," says Josephine.

"I can do it, Ma Mere. I just need to prepare for the worst. Having Cleo there will really help," Ora says.

"That's it, Ora. Cleo and Alexia will help to keep you calm," says Ellis.

"I have a really good feeling about Walmsley's speech. He'll finally show us who he really is tomorrow. You'll be there to witness it all unfold, Ora," Josephine says.

"I really don't know what to expect from Walmsley, but I'm sure it'll be more of the same Jim Crow charades. He's been Mayor for six years and it's been hard for us ever since. He cut your hours in half with the city and we've never really recovered, Ma Mere," Ora says.

"One day we'll be restored, Ora. Just listen to us and keep your mind clear. Walmsley will be gone before you know it and we'll be back on our feet," says Ellis.

"This summer has been so tough, looking for work and being rejected by everyone. I thought at least Alonzo would give me a chance, but now he's worried about school. I can't catch a break, Ma Mum," Ora says.

"Ora, it took me years to finally find my job with the city. Even working part time is a blessing. It will happen when you least expect it. Maybe once you return to school in the fall you'll get your first offer," says Josephine.

Ora takes a seat at the kitchen table. Ellis hands Ora

her mail. Ora begins to open the letters. She notices one letter from the state civil service division. She opens the letter quickly and says, "I've been waiting for this one."

"What you got there?" Josephine asks.

Ora reads the letter silently, then tosses it onto the kitchen table. "It's just another rejection letter from the state for an admin position. I really wish I could work for Governor Allen and Huey P. Long, but I just can't get hired. They said I'm too young," sulks Ora.

"That's alright, honey. You'll get 'em next time. Finish school and you'll get that state job right away, alright," consoles Ellis.

Just then, Cleo Lewis, Ora's younger brother walks through the front door. He's eight inches taller than Ora and strong. "Hey there, Ora. How'd it go today at Xavier?" asks Cleo.

"Xavier was great, but Alonzo's not ready to hire me yet," responds Ora.

"Ora, just give him some time. He'll hire you. Keep writing him and studying. Alonzo's just worried about you. That's all," Cleo says.

"Cleo, clean up for supper. We're having catfish and sweet potatoes tonight," says Josephine.

"You know that's my favorite. We can wait for Alexia though. Where is she, Ma Mere?" asks Cleo.

"Alexia is working as an assistant to Alonzo's mother doing seamstress work. She'll be home soon," replies Josephine.

"I didn't realize that Alexia had a job too. She's so young," says Cleo.

"Alexia enjoys design and fashion. It's just for the summer," says Josephine.

"Maybe she'll become a seamstress one day," suggests Ora.

"She can actually work in the evenings during school. It's a good skill to learn," says Josephine.

Alexia Lewis walks through the front door. She's wearing a yellow summer dress with white flowers. She's petite with a small frame. Her short brown hair is curly and neat. Alexia is carrying a baked apple pie. "Ma Mere and Ma Mum, I have a baked treat from Mrs. Willis," she says.

"The pie looks good, Alexia. Did you help her bake it?" asks Ellis.

"Actually, she prepared it this morning before I arrived," replies Alexia.

"Well, I'm definitely ready to taste the catfish, sweet

potatoes and apple pie," says Cleo.

"Don't forget the collard greens and cornbread, Cleo," says Ora. Everyone chuckles.

"Watermelon man, red to the rind!" shouts a fruit vendor passing by in his truck just outside the house.

"I can go grab a melon, Ma Mere. Would you like one?" offers Cleo.

"Buy two, Cleo," replies Josephine. Cleo rushes out to the street and buys the watermelons. He heads back inside quickly.

"I really wish your mom and dad were here now to see how you've grown up. They would be so proud of you," says Ellis.

"We certainly do miss them, but we love being here with you, Ma Mere and Ma Mum," Cleo says. Cleo takes a seat at the kitchen table beside Ora. Alexia sits down next to Cleo.

"Cleo, would you bless the food for us?" asks Ellis.

"Of course, Ma Mum," he replies. Everyone bows their heads. "God, we thank you for this meal and the blessing of our family. We pray for work to support us and for those less fortunate. Amen," prays Cleo.

"Amen," says Ora.

Ellis serves the food and Josephine helps her with the glasses. "Would anyone like some lemonade?" asks Josephine. Cleo pours lemonade into his glass, then passes the pitcher to Ora. Ora pours lemonade into her glass and into Alexia's glass.

"Thank you, Ora," says Alexia.

"Cleo, I'd like you and Alexia to join Ora tomorrow at a City Hall event. Mayor Walmsley is scheduled to give a speech," says Josephine.

"Do we have to? I really don't like Mayor Walmsley at all," replies Cleo.

"Mayor Walmsley is a bigot, Ma Mere," asserts Alexia.

"Ora needs the two of you there to support her. She's planning to cover Mayor Walmsley's speech for a letter to Alonzo Willis," says Josephine.

"Mayor Walmsley is so predictable. I can almost tell you what he's going to say before he says it," says Cleo.

"You never know, Cleo. Something unusual could happen tomorrow. Just go with Ora and you could actually experience something new," says Josephine.

"The only new thing that Mayor Walmsley has to say is that he hates Black people in a new evil way," Alexia

says.

"Ma Mere is right, Alexia and Cleo. I do need your support. Please join me tomorrow and I'll make it worth your while," says Ora.

"I don't know. It's just too little too late. What if something happens to us?" asks Cleo.

"Yeah, what if they attack us while we're there?" insists Alexia.

"I work for the city and nothing's ever happened to me. You'll be fine," says Josephine.

"You just be careful and pay attention. Everything should go well tomorrow," assures Ellis.

"We won't stay long. We just need to be there for Walmsley's speech," says Ora.

"Well, as long as we can get out of there quickly, it's alright with me," Cleo says.

"It shouldn't be too bad with all of us there together," says Alexia.

"Thank you, Cleo and Alexia. I won't let you down. When Alonzo does hire me, I'll take good care of you," promises Ora.

"That'll be the day!" exclaims Alexia.

"You owe me big time for this one, Ora," taunts

Cleo.

"Ora, was there any mention of Germany during Dr. Woodson's lecture?" asks Josephine.

"No, they just focused on segregation," Ora says.

"There's a reason that we speak German in this house. It's a reminder of what's good about the culture. Ora, I want you to study Adolf Hitler and the Nazis when you study Jim Crow. The system of racism is very important to understand," insists Josephine.

"When you understand the Nazis, you can prepare yourself to fight Jim Crow, Ora," adds Ellis.

"I've read about the burning books and the Jewish boycotts, but it's so confusing. Why do they attack their own German people who even fought in World War I?" asks Ora.

"Just as Jim Crow discriminates against us as Americans, even when we fight for our country, the Nazis single out the Jewish people. They've even stopped them from joining the German military," says Josephine.

"That's terrible, Ma Mere. The stories I've read about the book burnings remind me of lynchings. It's the same kind of hate," says Cleo.

"Germany never really recovered from the First

World War. The people are still fighting the enemy within," comments Ora.

"That's right, Ora. So, let's keep our eyes on Germany. We may have another war on our hands according to your dad," says Josephine.

"Papa is right. I just hope the Jewish people can survive Adolf Hitler," stresses Cleo.

"If it gets much worse, America may have to fight the Nazis," Ora says.

"America can barely fight its own battle against lynchings, murders and brutality of Black people. It will take a miracle for us to stand up to Nazi Germany," Josephine says.

"It's not impossible, but so many racist people already support the Nazis. When America fights the Nazis, something will break for Black people for the first time since the Civil War," says Ora.

"You're right on the money, Ora. It will be a breaking point for us," Ellis says.

"I read that Huey P. Long said today, 'Don't compare me to Hitler. He's a plain demon.' He would certainly fight Hitler if he were President," says Alexia.

"Huey P. Long has the sound mind and fairness to

stand up to segregation and the Nazis. He would give FDR a run for his money," says Josephine.

"Huey P. Long has been standing up to Mayor Walmsley and his Jim Crow politics for years. I'm surprised that Walmsley has survived the fight," says Ora.

"Walmsley was once backed by the Old Regulars who run every New Orleans campaign. Long defeated them to become governor, but they have a stronghold on the city," says Josephine.

"When Long defeats Walmsley, the city will be set free, even if it's still segregated for a while," says Ora.

"It's not so simple, Ora. Even Long has a lot of work to do to get rid of Jim Crow, but he's way ahead of his time," says Ellis.

"So, what's Walmsley's speech about? What kind of event is it?" asks Cleo.

"It's an address on the status of the city and its affairs including its weakening budget," replies Josephine.

"So, Mayor Walmsley wants to publicize his fight with Huey P. Long," surmises Cleo.

"Walmsley knows the people are waiting for a resolution to his battle with Senator Long, so he's going to raise the issues he's facing for the people," Ora says.

"Walmsley shouldn't have run for mayor again last year. Long should have stopped him," Alexia says.

"He still had so many supporters, even without the Old Regulars. We're in a defensive posture," Josephine says.

"Well, I'm ready to see Mayor Walmsley up close and in person, finally," says Ora.

"Don't get too close. He might single you out and catch you," says Cleo.

"You three must really be careful. We want you there, but you have to pay close attention to everything that's happening around you," says Josephine.

"We'll be careful, Ma Mere. There's no need to worry," assures Ora.

"Cleo, how was work today at McDonogh 35?" asks Ellis.

"It was pretty light, considering that we'll be back to school in two weeks," replies Cleo.

"That's a good job to have, even during school," says Josephine.

"I can work during the school year, but I won't earn very much money," complains Cleo.

"Every little bit helps," responds Josephine.

"What's on the radio tonight?" asks Ora.

"It's the usual news and music," says Ellis.

"I wish that Dr. Woodson's lecture was on the radio tonight," says Ora.

"One day the radio will have strong messages like that, but in 1935 the most we can get are Huey P. Long speeches," says Josephine.

"That's good enough for me!" exclaims Alexia. Everyone laughs.

"Ma Mum, when do you think Louisiana will desegregate? 1950? 1960?" asks Ora.

"Louisiana is so far away from desegregating, Ora. But I want you to dream of bringing desegregation to New Orleans. If you decide it will happen, then it will come to pass," replies Ellis.

"I'm only seventeen, Ma Mum. Whenever I try to make a difference I'm always discouraged. Will it ever turn around for me?" asks Ora.

"Just stay focused and work hard. Alonzo will take notice and people will listen to what you have to say, Ora," replies Ellis. She stands and walks over to Ora to give her a hug. "I love you so much. I believe in you, Ora," she says.

"We all believe in you," says Alexia.

Ora smiles and shrugs her shoulders. "I guess I can make a difference," she says.

"You can, but first of all let's see what you're wearing to the speech tomorrow. We don't want you to look down and out at City Hall," says Josephine.

"Ma Mere, I have no idea. My clothes are so dull. Do I really have to dress up for Mayor Walmsley's speech?" asks Ora.

"No, Ora. Just wear something nice. That goes for you too, Cleo and Alexia. Let me see what's in your closets," says Josephine.

Ora walks over to her bedroom. Her bed is made neatly and her books are stacked on her desk. Oddly, Ora notices that the glass of water at her bedside is half empty and a napkin is folded on the table. Ora knows that her grandmothers would have cleaned up the glass. Ora then realizes that her mother has entered her life again. "Mama? Are you still here?" Ora calls. She sits down on the edge of her bed and lifts the folded napkin to her cheek. "Mama, I miss you so much," cries Ora. Just then, one of Ora's books falls to the floor from her desk. Ora jumps slightly, then turns to the book. "Mama?" she calls.

"What are you doing in there?" asks Josephine,

walking into Ora's room.

"Mama's playing with me again, Ma Mere," replies Ora.

"Now, now don't get too excited. She's probably just a little worried about you tonight. Turn on your lantern and look for something nice to wear," insists Josephine. Ora reaches over to her lantern, then turns the nob to raise the flame. Ora turns to the closet and walks across the room. Suddenly the flame blows out.

"I see what's happening here, Ora. Let me get the lantern in the living room for you," says Josephine. She looks up to the ceiling and says, "Cecilia, Ora is frightened enough as it is. Don't scare the girl away." Josephine walks out to the hall toward the living room.

"What happened in there, Josephine? I saw the light blow out," asks Ellis.

"It's Cecilia again. She's trying to get Ora's attention for some reason, but I don't know why. I'm going to bring my big lantern in there and hope she doesn't blow out its flame as well," replies Josephine.

"I'm going to check on Ora," says Alexia. She walks down the hall to their room. "Are you alright in here?" asks Alexia.

"I'm fine. Mama has me in the dark tonight. Maybe she's upset about Walmsley," Ora says.

"You're right, Ora. Maybe we shouldn't go," says Alexia.

Josephine walks in and overhears Alexia. "You have to go tomorrow. Try not to worry too much about your mother. She's just trying to protect you from disappointment," explains Josephine.

"Cecilia was always like this when you were children. She'll calm down soon," adds Ellis.

Josephine replaces Ora's lantern with the larger lamp from the living room. She turns the nob to raise the flame. "There we go. Now let's see those outfits, girls," says Josephine.

Ora walks over to her closet and pulls out three dresses. Alexia reaches for four.

"This is what I had in mind," says Ora placing her dresses onto her bed. "I have a blue a-line, a red shift and a gray sheath," lists Ora.

"The gray sheath has the business style you need for City Hall. Try it on, so we can see how it fits," requests Josephine.

Ora takes off her white dress and pulls the gray

dress over her head. It fits loosely, because she is so small.

"There, Ora. That's much better. I'll take it in for you, because you've lost a little weight," offers Josephine.

"Thank you, Ma Mere. I don't know what I'd do without you," says Ora.

"I have a blue empire, a brown tent, a yellow apron dress and a white jumper dress," says Alexia.

"The blue empire dress might be best for you. Let's see it on you," Josephine says.

Alexia removes her yellow summer dress, then raises the blue dress to her chest. "Now that's the right style," laughs Alexia posing and prancing.

"Try it on, Alexia," says Ellis, peering through the door. Alexia wiggles her way into the dress. It fits just right. "Blue sure looks good on you, Alexia," says Ellis.

"Thank you, Ma Mum," says Alexia.

"I'll press it for you tonight, so it'll be just right," says Josephine.

"That would be great, Ma Mere," Alexia says.

"Well, ladies I'll take those dresses and get to work on them," says Josephine.

Ora and Alexia get undressed and hand their clothes to Josephine. They get ready for bed and place the remaining dresses back in their closets.

"Good night, Ora and Alexia," says Ellis.

"Good night, Ma Mum," says Ora and Alexia.

"I'll see you girls bright and early tomorrow morning," says Josephine as she leaves their room with the two dresses.

Ora sits down on her bed and reaches over to dim the lantern. It begins to dim on its own as the nob turns slowly. "Alexia, did you see that?" asks Ora.

"I saw you turn out the light," replies Alexia.

"It wasn't me. It was Mama again. I guess she's calmed down now," says Ora.

"Ora, I miss Mama so much. I wish that we could have seen her tonight," Alexia says.

"We just need to acknowledge her presence and understand her messages," Ora says.

"If she were here everything would be so different for us," says Alexia. She lies down in her bed beneath her covers.

Ora lies down too. "I try to imagine that Mama's here when I'm writing. It helps me escape the pain of rejection and hatred from segregation," says Ora.

"When I imagine she's here, I think about the time

we spent together during the holidays. She was such a beautiful person," reflects Alexia.

"Do you think I have what it takes to beat the system?" asks Ora.

"You're still learning, but you have the courage to beat the odds," replies Alexia. "What story will you write about tomorrow's speech?"

"Huey P. Long is on my mind, so I'll probably write about Walmsley's reaction to the Long restrictions," responds Ora.

"That's a good story. Alonzo should like your letter," Alexia says. "Well good night, Ora."

"Good night, Alexia," says Ora. Alexia and Ora both dim their lanterns and fall asleep.

CHAPTER 2 / "CLOSE COVERAGE"

"Good morning, Alexia and Ora. Your dresses are ready. Breakfast is on the table," says Josephine. Ora yawns and pulls down her covers. Alexia pulls her sheet over her head.

"Good morning, Ma Mere. Thank you," says Ora.

"Can I sleep for one more hour?" whines Alexia.

"Nope, it's time to get out of that bed," says Cleo as he walks by their room and pokes his head in the doorway. Cleo walks into the kitchen and sits down for breakfast. "Good morning, Ma Mum. I'll have the eggs, bacon, biscuits and orange juice," requests Cleo.

"Coming right up," replies Ellis.

"Maybe I can stay home today and help out around the house," says Alexia.

"You're going to miss it all. Please come with us, Alexia," insists Ora.

"Alexia, rise and shine. It's time to get dressed and eat breakfast," Josephine says.

Alexia throws the covers down and quickly sits up in her bed. "I'm up!" exclaims Alexia. She hops out of bed and takes her dress from Josephine.

"That's my girl," says Josephine.

Ora slips on her shoes and walks out to the kitchen. "The breakfast smells so good, Ma Mum," compliments Ora. She takes a seat next to Cleo. "So, what's on your mind this morning?"

"It's six thirty in the morning, Ora. There's not much to think about right now. I'm just hoping the day goes well," responds Cleo.

"That blue empire really brings out your shape. You look so nice today, Alexia," says Josephine.

"It even feels good. Thank you for pressing it, Ma Mere," says Alexia.

"Now let's get you some breakfast," says Josephine.

Alexia puts on her matching blue sandals and heads out to the kitchen. She takes a seat next to Cleo opposite Ora. "May I have bacon and eggs with coffee?" asks Alexia.

"Of course, honey. Would you like the usual cream and sugar?" replies Ellis.

"You know it, Ma Mum," says Alexia.

"So what time is Mayor Walmsley's speech today?" asks Cleo.

"His speech begins at ten o'clock. If you leave right at nine o'clock, you'll have just enough time to fight through the crowds on the streetcars and downtown. The conductors might put you off the cars when the seats fill with whites, but you can always catch the next one in time," says Josephine.

"In that case, maybe we should leave for eight just to be on the safe side," replies Ora.

"You can, but just be prepared to wait for a while at City Hall," says Josephine.

"Won't there be other speakers today?" asks Cleo.

"Yes, the Mayor's Deputy Commissioner of Public Finance, Henry Desmare will also speak on the city budget," says Josephine.

"That's pretty boring, Ma Mere," sulks Alexia.

"There's also a brief reporting on property taxes by Henry Umbach, President of the Board of Assessors," says Josephine.

"At least it's brief," says Cleo.

"It's all really important for my coverage. Let's leave at eight instead of nine. I want to make sure we don't miss a thing," Ora says.

"This is going to take forever," whines Alexia.

"It'll do you some good, Alexia. You can learn a thing or two," says Ellis.

"Just try to think about the bright side. Huey P. Long has Walmsley like a tiger by its tail. It won't be long before he throws in the towel," says Ora.

"What's in this morning's paper?" asks Cleo.

"It's all about Mayor Walmsley. He made the front page of the *Times Picayune*. They're really trying to give him a boost," replies Josephine.

"Nothing can make Walmsley look good. Not even for the whites who hate us," says Alexia.

"Alexia, I have a plan to finally stop Mayor Walmsley and bring an end to his evil ways," says Ora.

"What's that, Ora?" asks Cleo.

"I'm going to expose Mayor Walmsley's attacks on

Blacks and report them to Senator Long directly," replies Ora.

"That can be dangerous, Ora," says Alexia.

"Not if I work with Alonzo and Papa," Ora says.

"That's a good plan, Ora. I know you can do it, sweetie," says Josephine.

"What if Walmsley tries to stop you? What will you do?" asks Alexia.

"Alonzo will know what to do. I'll take my time and cover my tracks," Ora says.

"Let's get you hired by Alonzo first and work on Walmsley once you're in place," suggests Cleo. "Let me see this morning's newspaper."

Josephine walks over to the living room and picks up the newspaper from the chaise. She hands the paper to Cleo.

"Thank you, Ma Mere. Now let's see. Here it is. Walmsley front and center. With all the news from Washington and FDR, the city is under siege today," says Cleo.

"There's so much turmoil with Huey P. Long that we have to pay close attention to Walmsley, even if he is a segregationist," says Ora.

"I want you to look for anything you can about segregation during the event today. Notice who's holding up any signs or picking any fights. Long's men will likely be there today, so keep your eyes open," says Josephine.

"I remember when I was your age. We were so afraid to go downtown. The city was so clouded by fear. I barely made it through those days. Thank God I'm alive," says Ellis.

"The threat of lynching must have frightened you half to death, Ma Mum," Ora says.

"That's right, Ora. We never went out at night or wandered off by ourselves. It was a terrible time," replies Ellis. "Eventually things settled down, but I'll never forget how it felt to live in constant fear."

"I wish that I was as brave as you, Ma Mum," states Ora.

"You have it in you, Ora. Just look beyond the disappointments and the fear to see yourself for who you truly can be," says Ellis.

"It's just so hard for girls, especially Black girls to be anything more than a shadow. It's so hard to break free," says Ora.

"Ora, just imagine if you had to find a job as a

servant at your age. Do you realize how discouraging it would be for you as a writer?" asks Ellis.

"I understand. A lot of girls have to quit school for work like that. It's not fair at all," replies Ora.

"It wouldn't be fair to you, Cleo or Alexia for you to give up writing just to make a few extra dollars here and there. But it also means that you have to work ten times harder to survive as a writer," says Ellis.

"I wouldn't mind working as a servant," says Alexia.

"You are a servant, girl. Pick up these plates," laughs Cleo.

"That's not funny!" shouts Alexia.

"You kids settle down and get ready to head out soon. Here's the fare for the streetcar," says Josephine. She hands one dollars in change to Ora.

"Thank you, Ma Mere," Ora says.

"It's fifteen minutes to eight. We've prepared your lunch for you. It's there on the counter," offers Ellis. She hands a bag to Alexia filled with packed sandwiches and fresh fruit.

"This looks really good," says Alexia.

"You shouldn't be too hungry with what I've

packed," says Ellis.

"I know what I'm looking for and I know why we're going, but I just don't know what to expect," says Ora.

"Ora, today will be a turning point for you and your writing. Believe in yourself and stay focused. You will write your best letter yet," Josephine says.

"I trust you and Ma Mum, even if the speech is uneventful and I don't find anything I'm looking for. Just being there today will make me a much better writer," says Ora.

"Ora, you ever looked in the obituary section of the newspaper? There are a lot more Black deaths than whites these days. Makes it seem like something else is going on. Like we're a target. You know?" comments Alexia.

"Let me see the newspaper, Cleo," says Ora. Cleo hands the morning edition of the *Times Picayune* to Ora. Ora flips the pages to the obituaries. She turns to Alexia and says, "You're right about one thing. Blacks are dying of heart attacks and pneumonia more than others. There are one to two murders, but they're mostly natural causes."

"Come on ladies. It's eight o'clock. Let's get going before it's too late," says Cleo.

"You're right, Cleo. Let's head out now," Ora says.

Alexia grabs the lunch bag in the kitchen, then heads to the front door. Ora follows Alexia. Cleo opens the front door for Alexia and Ora.

"Bye, Ma Mere and Ma Mum. We'll be back before you know it," says Ora.

"Try to stay focused," says Josephine. She watches as Ora, Cleo and Alexia walk down Annette Street toward Claiborne Avenue.

"We have to hurry. It's a long walk to the streetcars," says Cleo.

"We're making good time," replies Ora.

"I feel like we're in a big rush," says Alexia.

"Just try to keep up, Alexia," scolds Cleo.

"If we can make it to Canal Street, we might not have to take a streetcar or deal with the race screens and white crowds," says Ora.

"That would be nice, but it's such a long walk," replies Alexia.

"Hey, where you going this morning, Ora?" asks their neighbor Ronald Broussard, waving and smiling.

"We're headed to City Hall to hear Mayor Walmsley's speech," replies Cleo.

"Well, be careful and let me know how it goes

today," says Ronald. He heads back inside and closes the door behind him.

"Mr. Broussard watches everything. He's got eyes like a hawk," says Cleo.

"Sometimes I wonder if he ever has time to work," says Alexia.

"He's a laborer. He works at night. I've seen him come home early in the mornings," says Ora.

"I never knew that. I always assumed that he just had his own business," says Cleo.

"No, he just works really hard, Cleo," says Ora. "We have one more block to go before we reach Claiborne. Let's watch out for the traffic," she continues. Two cars pass slowly by. Cleo, Ora and Alexia cross over to the right side of the street.

"What if Mayor Walmsley doesn't allow Blacks in beyond a certain point? Should we just turn around and go home?" asks Alexia.

"We'll get close enough to hear Mayor Walmsley and see the people's reactions to his speech," replies Ora.

"Will that really be enough?" asks Alexia.

"It will have to do for now," responds Ora. They turn right onto Claiborne Avenue. The street is busy with oncoming traffic. Men and women are dressed in business attire and rushing to work. There are a handful of children and teenagers in the busy crowd. The fortunate Black people with a car have several carpooling passengers to try to beat the summer heat.

"I wish we had a car," says Alexia.

"Cars are so expensive and you can't even find gas in the segregated areas of the city. They're nice to have, but they're tough to maintain," says Ora.

"It's pretty much the same everywhere you go. It's segregated and you just can't have freedom," says Cleo. They make it to Esplanade Avenue. The neighborhoods are a few steps up from Annette Street. Many houses have beveled glass windows and driveways for the bounty of cars. The families are well off, but modest in this predominately Black area.

"Freedom dwells in your imagination, Cleo. You can transcend segregation in your mind and in your heart," says Ora.

"You've been reading too many college books, Ora. We can't escape Jim Crow. He's everywhere," says Alexia.

"That's exactly what they want you to believe, Alexia. Ora is right that we can escape segregation in our minds," says Cleo.

"When you realize that they can only take the parts of your life that you give to them like your education and dreams for your future, you live a new reality," says Ora. They reach Orleans Avenue. This section of the city is one of the oldest. The streets are bustling with residents and tourists alike. Restaurants and bars line the blocks. The smell of freshly baked French bread and hot coffee fills the morning air.

"When I finish school, I'm going to be a seamstress, designing wedding gowns and ball gowns. Jim Crow won't stop me," says Alexia.

"That's right, Alexia," assures Ora.

"No matter what, they'll always be something that'll try and stop us, but we have to be ready and make up our minds to fight it," says Cleo.

"It's segregation now, but one day it'll be something bigger, maybe a war. Who knows, Alexia," speculates Ora.

"I just wish we could escape it all today," says Alexia.

"Try to imagine our lives without segregation and Jim Crow violence," says Ora.

"I'm trying, but I just can't see beyond today," says

Alexia.

"That's alright, little sister. Before you know it, this will all be over and you'll have the freedom that you dream of," says Ora.

"Yeah, one day," says Alexia.

"Don't get so down, Alexia. It's like Papa always says, you must take pride in being Black," says Cleo. They arrive at Canal Street. The streetcars pass by slowly just as they make it there. The area is predominately white. White motorists drive by quickly as they take it all in.

"Let's try to take the streetcar to Saint Charles and walk to Gallier Hall from there," suggests Ora.

"Ora, maybe we should just walk to Gallier Hall from here. It's only nine o'clock," replies Cleo.

"If we take the streetcar, we'll be fresh when we get there," says Alexia.

A streetcar pulls in to their stop and slows down. The loud screeching sound fills the summer air. The conductor opens the door. "Are you boarding?" he asks. Cleo turns to Ora for approval, then responds, "Yes we are." Cleo steps aboard the streetcar, then deposits the needed change. Ora follows Cleo and does the same. Alexia climbs aboard, and gives her change to Cleo.

"Head to the rear and stand up. These seats are for whites only," commands the conductor.

Cleo marches solemnly to the back of the streetcar followed by Ora and Alexia. The streetcar is filled with white passengers. There are no Black people aboard. Race screens line the back seats.

"Get out of here you negra," mumbles one angry passenger.

"Yeah, just get!" says another. The angry passenger shoves Cleo in the back.

"Hey, watch out," says Cleo.

"Settle down back there!" shouts the conductor as he starts the streetcar back down Canal Street.

Cleo, Ora, and Alexia stand in the rear of the streetcar holding on to the upright wooden beams.

"It won't be long before we're there, Cleo. I'm sorry," consoles Ora.

"I'm used to it now, Ora. That's alright," replies Cleo.

"I'm just glad we're here now instead of out there walking," says Alexia.

The conductor pulls in to the next stop on South Robertson Street. A family of three stands at the stop waiting to board. They're white. "That's it, you three. You have to get off here," the conductor shouts.

"What? We just got on," cries Alexia. The white family boards the streetcar and walks toward the rear.

Ora motions to Cleo and Alexia. "Let's go," she says. Ora steps down onto the ground pushing through the back doors. Cleo and Alexia follow her.

"I can't believe that. He put us off and stole our fare," says Alexia.

"We shouldn't have gotten on the streetcar. We should have walked all the way to Gallier Hall instead," says Ora.

"Well, now we know better. When the streetcar is full of whites, stay far way," says Cleo.

"It's just a busy day. We'll catch the streetcar some other time," says Ora. She extends her hand for Alexia to hold. "Are you alright, girl?" asks Ora.

"I'm fine. It's just those hateful people that get the best of me," replies Alexia.

"You're doing really well considering the streetcar mess. I know your legs are tired, but try to hold on," says Ora.

"We'll be there soon, Alexia," says Cleo.

"We're going to walk down to Saint Charles Avenue and walk right to Gallier Hall," says Ora.

"If we hurry, we can be there in time for the event to begin," says Cleo. "We should just barely make it." Canal Street is filled with lively thriving shops and businesses. As they walk along the sidewalk, they move quickly to avoid the whites in front of them. They often jump down to the street from the sidewalk to make room. All of the shops have signs displayed that forbid Blacks from entering. Alexia glances at the shops and frowns as she realizes that she'll never be allowed in.

Ora looks straight ahead and barely notices the shops or Jim Crow signs. She's focused and eager to finally see Mayor Walmsley in the flesh. Cleo walks on the edge of the sidewalk near the street to avoid making contact with whites at all. He's so used to being pushed and hit by whites that avoidance is his only defense. Some of the people stop and stare at Cleo and especially Alexia, because she's so small and she seems so out of place. Ora stares back at them when they get too close. Alexia tries not to notice the people and their hostilities. She sometimes grabs Ora's hand to catch up and keep herself from getting lost in the crowd.

"Papers! Get your papers! Mayor Walmsley speaks today at City Hall!" shouts the newspaper stand owner. A small group of people flock to the newsstand to take a look at the front page. They point and chat about the day's news. Cleo holds Ora and Alexia to block the group of onlookers from knocking them over. "Let's move fast. The crowd is getting hectic," says Cleo. "If we can just make it to Saint Charles Avenue."

"We're only three blocks away. I know it's hard, but we're almost there," says Ora.

"We're going to be a little late," mentions Cleo. "It's already nine forty-five," looking down at his watch.

"It might take us another twenty minutes, but we should arrive just in time for the introduction," estimates Ora. They begin to rush. They breeze past the oncoming crowd and figuratively take flight. Alexia begins to look past the shops. Cleo moves onto the sidewalk and Ora leads the way. Cleo holds Ora's small frail hand at times and keeps her moving ahead.

"Excuse me," says Ora to the people as they pass by. Many whites shove the three of them and call them names, but they ignore the meanness. "Finally, Saint Charles Avenue. We can get past this Canal Street crowd."

The opulent architecture on Saint Charles Avenue is picturesque and other worldly for Ora, Cleo and Alexia. It's not their first time there, but it's such a major contrast to their Annette Street home. The pulse of Saint Charles is altogether different than Canal. The cars whizz by on nearly empty streets. There are very few shops and mostly office buildings on the avenue. They stroll down the street free from the constant reminders of Jim Crow segregation. Very rarely do they see signs banning them from entering the stately buildings.

"We've finally arrived. I wouldn't mind walking on Saint Charles any day," says Cleo.

"Look out ahead, Cleo. We'll be back in the crowd in a couple of blocks, so get ready," says Ora. They reach Gravier Street and begin to notice a few more pedestrians than usual. They're polite businessmen who don't push or mistreat them. "Good morning," says Ora to one man. He nods politely.

"It's five minutes to ten," says Cleo glancing at his watch.

"We're about ten minutes away at this pace. Let's hurry," says Ora. They rush down the street toward Gallier Hall.

"I can't keep up with you, Ora. Slow down," urges Alexia.

Ora stops for a moment, then takes Alexia's hands and turns toward her. "You can do this. I promise I'll treat you to something nice if you just walk as fast as you can. We're so close now, Alexia," says Ora.

"We really need you this time. Just try your best, alright," urges Cleo.

"I'll try, but slow down a little," pleads Alexia.

"We're one block away from the event. You can make it, Alexia," encourages Ora. They see a massive crowd up ahead. Gallier Hall has been transformed for Mayor Walmsley's speech. Confederate banners are draped along a large outdoor stage that covers the front steps of Gallier Hall. Horse mounted police and officers on motor bikes heavily patrol the swelling crowd. They finally make it to Lafayette Square just across from City Hall. Ora looks through the crowd for familiar faces and notices Doctor Claude Batiste, a Black physician. "Cleo and Alexia, follow me," says Ora.

"What is it?" asks Cleo.

"I see a friend I'd like to introduce to you," replies Ora. The festivities have nearly begun. A band plays "Dixie

Land" to signal the beginning of the event as Mayor Walmsley, Henry Umbach and Henry Desmare march onto the stage. Mayor Walmsley waves and smiles at the cheering crowd below.

"Dr. Batiste, hello," says Ora, reaching over to touch the doctor's arm.

Dr. Batiste turns to Ora in surprise. "Hi there, Ora," he says.

"I'd like to introduce you to my sister Alexia and my brother Cleo," says Ora.

"It's very nice to meet the two of you. I know Ora from Xavier. She's there so often," responds Dr. Batiste. It's hard for them to hear with the excitement from the crowd and the music. Cleo and Alexia lean in closer.

"We decided to make the trip yesterday. It's a long walk from home, but we finally made it here," says Ora.

"That's a good trip to make. Ora, excuse me. I see officials from the Charity Hospital Board who I need to meet. I'll just be right over there," explains Dr. Batiste pointing to the opposite side of Saint Charles.

"We understand, Dr. Batiste. We're going to find some room in our section closer to Gallier Hall," says Ora.

"Alright, Ora. It's good to see you again," says Dr.

Batiste as he walks closer to Gallier Hall and the section reserved for special guests. He knows that he's not allowed in the section, but he hopes to get the attention of the Charity Hospital Board members from the outside.

Ora watches as Dr. Batiste makes his way over to Gallier Hall. She notices where he stands, then turns to Cleo and Alexia. "Let's find a spot across the street," says Ora.

"We can get a lot closer if we do. We'll see everything we need to in the Black section on the left," says Cleo. They make their way through the heart of the crowd over to the left edge designated for Black people. They begin to notice a group of men in suits surrounding the Black gathering. They also notice casually dressed bullies staring the men down. The bullies are noticeably positioned near the stage and surrounding the section reserved for whites only.

"There's something unusual happening here today," says Cleo.

"Cleo, if it's the men in suits you're worried about, try not to. They're Huey P. Long's men. They always appear when Walmsley makes a public spectacle of himself," says Ora.

"So, you know who they are?" asks Alexia, wondering if Ora is aware of some kind of danger.

"I've studied a lot about Walmsley. His men are plainclothes Jim Crow lynchers just waiting to hurt one of us," says Ora.

"So why did we come today if they're so dangerous?" asks Alexia.

"Long's men are here to protect us. We should be safe out here," replies Ora.

"Let go of my son!" yells John Smith, Sr. as Walmsley's men apprehend him, his son and his wife. The crowd of Black people suddenly turns their attention to the Smith family and gasps.

"Get back now!" screams one of Walmsley's men to John Smith, Sr.

Suddenly, two of Long's men reach for John Smith, Jr. "Let go of the boy now and there won't be any trouble!" demands one of Long's men who pulls out his pistol and points it toward Walmsley's men. Ora, Alexia and Cleo are within feet of the melee. One of Walmsley's men quickly reacts, pulling out his pistol and shooting John Smith, Jr. in his left thigh. "Bang!" The sharp sound of the pistol snaps through the melodies in the festive air. Everyone in the crowd runs for cover. Mayor Walmsley is quickly lead back into City Hall with his staff. The police rush to capture the shooter and control the overwhelming crowd. The music stops and the press grabs for any hint of coverage and photographs they can. Long's men protect the Smith family from gunfire and Walmsley's men. Ora runs over to the Smith family to assist them. The police refuse to offer aid to John Smith, Jr.

"He needs a doctor! Please help us!" screams Ann Smith, John's mother.

"I can help you. Try to hold on," says Ora. Cleo and Alexia are stunned. Their worst nightmare is unfolding before their eyes. Ora runs over to Dr. Claude Batiste for help through the frantic crowd. He's startled by the gunshot, but he's alert. "Dr. Batiste, please save the boy who was shot. The police will not help him," pleads Ora.

"I'm coming right now. Did they catch the shooter?" asks Dr. Batiste.

"They caught him, and it's safe now. I witnessed it all," replies Ora.

"Thank God you're alive," says Dr. Batiste. He and Ora run over to the Smith family.

"He's a physician," explains Ora. Long's men make

room for Dr. Batiste.

"We have to stop the bleeding," Dr. Batiste says. He applies pressure to John Smith, Jr.'s large wound. The press pushes their way through to get a view of John Smith, Jr.

"Back up!" shouts one of Long's men.

"Cleo, we need an ambulance," urges Dr. Batiste. "Can you find one for us?"

"I'm on my way now. I won't waste a second, Dr. Batiste," replies Cleo. He runs down Saint Charles Avenue looking for help. He enters a hotel despite the sign banning Blacks from entering. "Please help. We need an ambulance," pleads Cleo.

"We heard about the shooting. Where are the police?" asks the desk clerk.

"They refuse to help," responds Cleo. "Can you call Charity Hospital?" requests Cleo.

"We're not supposed to get involved, but we know it's an emergency. We'll make a call," says the desk clerk.

"Thank you! Thank you," says Cleo.

"Hello? There's been a shooting," says the desk clerk to the Charity triage nurse.

"How many were injured?" asks the triage nurse.

"How many were injured?" the desk clerk asks Cleo.

"One young boy was shot in his left thigh. He's in front of Gallier Hall," replies Cleo.

"A Negro boy was shot in his left thigh. Please send an ambulance to Gallier Hall," says the desk clerk.

"It's on the way," assures the triage nurse.

"Thank you," says Cleo. "You might have saved his life."

The desk clerk hangs up the phone. "Let's keep this between us. You're not supposed to be here," says the desk clerk.

"I understand. I'm leaving now," says Cleo. He exits the hotel quickly, then runs back over to Ora. "The ambulance is on its way."

"Thank you, Cleo. I knew you could do it," says Ora. Alexia gravitates over to Cleo after watching the tragedy unfold in shock.

"Alexia, are you alright?" asks Cleo. Alexia doesn't respond. The bloody scene is too much for her delicate mind to handle. Cleo pulls Alexia closer to him, then hugs her.

Alexia begins to sob. "Why did we come to City

Hall? I can't believe this happened," cries Alexia.

"It's alright, Alexia. We had no idea," consoles Ora.

"Cleo, can you get me some bandages?...No, never mind. There's nothing to buy in this area," says Dr. Batiste.

"Here's my jacket. You can use it to tie around John's leg," says John Smith, Sr. "Is he going to be alright?"

"If the ambulance arrives soon, he'll be much better by tonight," says Dr. Batiste.

Cleo sees the emergency driver pull into the area. "There's the ambulance. Let me show them how to get here," says Cleo as he dashes off to the wandering truck. Cleo reaches the ambulance and directs the driver to the Smith's. "The shooting victim is in front of Gallier Hall with a doctor. Can you reach them?" asks Cleo.

"We may have to carry him to the truck. We're headed over to him now," the driver says as he climbs out of the ambulance with the medic. Cleo walks the driver and medic over to John Smith, Jr. and Dr. Batiste.

"You arrived just in time. He's lost so much blood," says Dr. Batiste.

"The bad news is that we have to carry your son to the ambulance," says the driver.

"He could just barely make it without losing consciousness," says Dr. Batiste.

"Alright, parents, can we lift him and carry him now?" asks the medic.

"Let's do it," says John Smith, Sr. Ann Smith holds her son's hand tightly. "You can do it, son. You'll be at the hospital before you know it," John says.

John Smith, Jr. cries out as his parents lift his wounded body. "Please slow down. It hurts! It hurts!" he cries.

Dr. Batiste and the medic slow their pace to comfort John Smith, Jr. "Is that better?" asks Dr. Batiste.

"It feels like I'm dying," replies John Smith, Jr. Ora, Cleo and Alexia follow the Smith's to the ambulance. When they arrive, Dr. Batiste gingerly places John Smith, Jr. onto the stretcher. He and the Smith's climb into the ambulance. The medic places bandages on John Smith, Jr.'s wound.

"Thank you, Ora and Cleo. You may have saved his life," says Dr. Batiste.

"Yes, thank you," says Mr. and Mrs. Smith waving goodbye.

"We're praying for you. Take care," says Ora. The

medic secures the ambulance doors closed and they drive around Lafayette Square to Poydras Street. Ora, Alexia and Cleo walk back over to Gallier Hall. A good number of the people in the crowd remain in the area even as an announcement is made that Mayor Walmsley's speech has been cancelled.

"Today's event has come to an end due to the violent incident," says the master of ceremonies. "Please disperse for your own safety."

"Cleo and Alexia, I need to speak with the men who fought with the shooter," says Ora.

"Take your time," says Cleo. Alexia shrugs her shoulders and follows Cleo.

Ora approaches Long's men and says, "I'm Ora Lewis and I'm covering today's shooting. May I ask you a few questions?"

"Ora, the men you saw here today were members of the White League, a group of killers who follow Mayor Walmsley," one of Long's men reveals.

"Do you know the name of the shooter?" asks Ora.

The men nod their heads in unison. "No, we can't identify them yet. The police should know more soon," they say.

"Could you provide your names?" inquires Ora.

"What was the name of your paper? Where do you work?" one of the men asks.

"I'm with the Sepia Socialite," replies Ora.

Cleo and Alexia turn away and look at each other in embarrassment. "She's really asking for it," says Alexia.

"If she digs any deeper, she'll be in a hole she can't escape," says Cleo. Alexia chuckles.

"Excuse us, Ora. We have a big mess to clean up here," says one of the men pointing down to John Smith, Jr.'s blood on the sidewalk.

"I understand," says Ora. The men turn to each other and begin discussing the shooting. Ora moves toward Cleo and Alexia. "I can't believe they spoke with me. I wanted more details, but they said a lot," says Ora.

"You've got to be careful about telling them you're a journalist. You wouldn't want Alonzo to be upset with you, would you, Ora?" asks Cleo.

"Try not to worry about Alonzo. After today, he'll be proud to hear from us," replies Ora. "Let me speak with some of the witnesses before they leave, Cleo and Alexia."

"We'll wait over here for you," says Cleo.

Ora walks over to a Black couple standing near

Long's men. "Good morning. My name is Ora Lewis and I'm a writer. I'd like to ask you about what you witnessed here today," says Ora.

"Hello, Ora," responds the man. "My name is Charles Allen and this is my wife Sally. We know the Smith's," says Charles.

Ora extends her hand to Charles and Sally. "It's very nice to meet you, Mr. and Mrs. Allen."

Charles and Sally shake Ora's hand. "Ora, John Smith, Sr. was a city employee. He was here today to ask to be rehired. Walmsley fired hundreds of Black workers and John was one of them," reveals Charles.

"I see, Mr. Allen. What triggered the argument?" asks Ora.

"After John picked up his severance check from City Hall, the clerks pointed him out for arguing about being fired. Walmsley's men grabbed John, Jr. and the fight began," says Charles.

Alonzo Willis arrives at City Hall expecting to catch Mayor Walmsley's speech. He walks toward the stage, then stops to greet a young couple who are fans of his writing. "Alonzo Willis? Hi there. Can you believe what happened today?" asks Alfred Brown.

"I arrived minutes ago. What's going on?" asks Alonzo.

"Alonzo, a small boy was shot. Mayor Walmsley's speech was cancelled," explains Alfred. Alonzo looks over in the direction of the shooting site, where Alfred is pointing. Alonzo notices Ora, Cleo and Alexia in the frenzied crowd. "A girl and her brother helped to save the boy's life," says Alfred.

"That would be Ora," responds Alonzo. He says, "It's good to see you. Take care," as he trots over to Ora on the opposite side of Saint Charles. "Ora Lewis, I'm hearing stories about you, girl," says Alonzo, interrupting her interview of the witnesses.

Ora turns to Alonzo in complete surprise. "Mr. Willis? How did you know we were here?" asks Ora.

"I didn't know until I arrived a moment ago. I planned to be here for Mayor Walmsley's speech," replies Alonzo.

"Oh, Mr. Willis, this is Charles and Sally Allen," says Ora.

"Nice to meet you, Charles and Sally," says Alonzo nodding his head.

"We were just discussing the argument that incited

the shooting," says Ora.

"Have you heard about the shooting?" asks Charles.

"I only know that the victim was a small boy," replies Alonzo.

"His name is John Smith, Jr. He and his parents are friends of ours. Ora can tell you the story we've shared with her. We've actually got to get going," says Charles, looking at Sally. Sally agrees with Charles.

"I understand. I'm very sorry this happened to your friends, the Smith's," says Alonzo. Charles and Sally leave quickly and walk toward the streetcar. Alonzo turns to Ora. "I can't believe that you witnessed an actual shooting, Ora," he says.

Cleo and Alexia walk over to Ora when they see Alonzo. "Hello, Alonzo. We're glad to see you here," says Cleo.

"Hi there, Cleo and Alexia. I was just telling your sister how glad I was that the three of you were here to see the shooting," says Alonzo.

"I've never seen anything like this before," says Alexia.

"Hopefully, we'll never see another small Black boy being shot again," says Ora. "The police refused to help him, because he was Black. Cleo had to find a phone to call an ambulance from the hospital."

"Ora, you three must be exhausted. Would you like a ride home?" offers Alonzo.

"Of course, Alonzo. We walked all the way here from Annette Street. The streetcar put us off, because we were Black after just one block," replies Ora.

"Well, let's walk to my car and get you out of here," says Alonzo.

"I don't know if I could have made it home walking the entire way," says Alexia.

"I'm glad I found you just in time," Alonzo says. "Follow me. I parked on Camp Street." They cross over to Lafayette Square, then head left down Camp Street. The streets are very busy and crowded with people curious to see the rumored shooting scene. Despite the traffic, they make it quickly to Alonzo's car. There's a red flag on Alonzo's windshield. "Oh no! Another parking ticket," says Alonzo. He grabs the ticket and shoves it into his pocket. "That's the third one this summer."

"I'm sorry, Alonzo. What did you do wrong?" asks Ora.

"They write them, because I'm Black. There's no

other reason. When the white hotel owners see me, they call the meter maids," explains Alonzo.

"That's so unfair. It's almost as bad as the streetcars," says Ora.

"I want a car, but it's so hard for Black people to drive," says Cleo.

Alonzo opens the car door for Ora, then he opens the driver's side doors. "Hop in," says Alonzo. They climb into Alonzo's car. Alonzo turns the key to his ignition. "I see the lunch bag that Alexia has, but you three must have worked up a real appetite. Would you like to have lunch at my mother's? Louise is there preparing the meal," offers Alonzo.

"That would be very nice," replies Ora.

"I know you're working for my mother this summer, Alexia, but don't worry. You can relax today. Just wait 'til Louise hears about this," says Alonzo.

"If you hadn't come, I'd probably still be there questioning witnesses," says Ora.

"How do you feel right now? Do you feel that something different is happening to your thoughts?" asks Alonzo.

"I feel like everything I studied has prepared me for

this moment, like my life has now changed forever," replies Ora earnestly.

"I think that today was very dangerous, but it turned out better in the end," responds Alexia.

"My thoughts are still racing. I can't make up my mind. We did so much to save John Smith, Jr. so quickly. I'm at peace now," replies Cleo.

"That's it. That's your inspiration to be a writer or to bring change where it's needed most, in the city, in the parishes, in your schools. The three of you are now real leaders," urges Alonzo.

"I hope this means that you'll accept my letters from now on," says Ora.

"Letters? I'm thinking articles one day, Ora. It will take time, but with instincts like yours, you'll be a writer soon. I'd even like to write an article about the three of you myself," says Alonzo.

"I don't know what to say, Alonzo. You know how long I've waited for this day when you would begin to trust my writing," says Ora.

"Your instincts in knowing where to be and what to do at just the right time have definitely developed, Ora," says Alonzo. "We can build your writing skills. We just needed to know that you had it in you."

"Ora really did insist that we all be here for Walmsley's speech. She knew to be early," chimes in Cleo.

"If you'd arrived ten minutes later, you would have missed it all," says Alonzo. He turns left onto Canal Street. The traffic is backed up from the City Hall crowd. There's a great deal of confusion about the safety of Mayor Walmsley. False rumors quickly spread about the shooting and the remaining dangers.

"It was Walmsley's men who attacked the boy and his parents," reveals Ora.

"How can you be so sure, Ora?" asks Alonzo.

"I spoke with Long's men who confronted the shooter with guns. They identified them as a group of killers from the White League who follow Walmsley closely," replies Ora.

"That's what I suspected, but I didn't want to jump to conclusions," says Alonzo. "What else did the men share?"

"They only said that the police would know more about the shooter. They refused to share their identities," Ora replies.

Alonzo finally makes it through the heavy traffic

and turns right onto Claiborne Avenue. There aren't as many people on the streets and Alonzo zips toward Elysian Fields Avenue. "Ora, we have a lot of work to do to cover this story. This will be your first article and the first feature story about you in the Sepia Socialite," says Alonzo.

"The men were so forceful and so angry with each other. They were ready to kill at any moment's notice," says Ora.

"That's good. That's the kind of detail we'll need for the story," assures Alonzo.

"We saw Long's men pull out their guns. We were so afraid," says Cleo.

"I'm sure you were. So how did you save the boy?" asks Alonzo.

"What we did was provide the doctor and the ambulance when the police refused to help," replies Ora.

"How did you find a doctor in that frantic crowd?" inquires Alonzo.

"Doctor Claude Batiste was there today to hear Mayor Walmsley's speech. We greeted him on our way there," replies Ora.

"Doctor Batiste didn't hesitate to care for the boy," says Cleo.

"Claude is a friend of mine. This is really good news," says Alonzo.

"Everyone knows that Dr. Batiste saved the day," says Cleo.

"So many reporters will try to reach him, but he may be relieved to hear from me," says Alonzo.

"He mentioned something about meeting the Charity Hospital Board members today. Now that he's rescued John Smith, Jr. as a Charity Hospital patient, the Board is sure to notice him," says Ora.

"Claude. He's always been so ambitious. He finally has the attention he deserves," shares Alonzo.

"He can't be ignored now," says Cleo.

Alonzo turns left down Elysian Fields Avenue. The neighborhood is modest and well maintained. There are a good number of cars on the streets as well as pedestrians.

"I'll give Claude a call tomorrow to ask for an interview and photographs," Alonzo says.

"I can write about several aspects of today's incident, including Dr. Batiste. May I also interview him?" asks Ora.

"Of course you can, Ora," replies Alonzo. He pulls up to the front of his mother's home on North Tonti Street.

"Well, here we are. Come on inside," says Alonzo. He opens his car door for Alexia. Cleo and Ora follow Alonzo into the house. They can smell the freshly fried chicken and baked rolls from the front door. "Mama, Louise, I've invited three guests for lunch today," says Alonzo.

"Hi Alexia, Ora and Cleo. How are you today?" asks Alonzo's mother Jimmie.

"Come on in and take a seat. Lunch is ready," says Louise, Alonzo's wife.

"Thank you, Mrs. Willis and Louise. Everything looks so good," says Ora.

"The three of them have had a very long day already," says Alonzo.

"We're so glad you made it back from City Hall considering the shooting. We heard about it on the radio and started praying for you," says Louise.

"Louise, I missed the entire thing, because I was late. Ora, Cleo and Alexia helped to save the boy's life," explains Alonzo.

"Really?" asks Louise and Jimmie in surprise.

"We found Doctor Claude Batiste just in time for the boy and Cleo called an ambulance," replies Alexia. Ora and Cleo have a seat at the table. Alexia walks over to

Jimmie.

"Have a seat and relax, Alexia. I know you must be flustered," says Jimmie. Alexia sits down next to Ora.

"So you witnessed the whole thing?" asks Louise.

"We were right there front and center," says Cleo.

"Louise, we're covering the three of them in a feature story, along with Doctor Batiste," says Alonzo.

"This is big news, Alonzo. It's exactly the kind of story we've been waiting for," says Louise.

"Alonzo, bless the meal for us," says Jimmie.

"Of course, mother," Alonzo replies, bowing his head. "Lord, we thank you for this nourishment and for our safety. Amen," he prays. Jimmie takes a seat next to Alonzo.

Louise serves the food. "We have fried chicken, green beans and mashed potatoes. The rolls are here as well," she says.

Cleo helps himself to the fried chicken. Ora takes a little bit of everything. Alexia is shy and doesn't eat much.

"Alexia, what's the matter?" asks Jimmie.

"I had a feeling that Mayor Walmsley was trouble and I wanted to stay home, but I went along anyway," says Alexia.

"Well, you got to see Jim Crow in action for yourself. You have to learn sometime," says Jimmie.

"It could have been much worse. It's alright. I'm just still anxious," says Alexia.

"I'm so sorry this happened, Alexia. I won't ever put you in this kind of situation again," says Ora.

"You shouldn't blame yourself, Ora," says Louise.

"I knew Long's men would be there and Walmsley's men would oppose them. I shouldn't have insisted that Alexia come," says Ora.

"Ora, Alexia is young, but she should experience what it really means to be Black in 1935. She can't hide from hatred," say Jimmie. Alexia looks over at Jimmie and nods her head.

"She'll be fine. Just give her some time," says Cleo.

"So what did the news report on the radio?" asks Alonzo.

"They said that there was an attack and that police were investigating. They said Mayor Walmsley was safe, but that he was very upset. He blamed the victim for the shooting," replies Louise.

"Typical Walmsley rhetoric. He just can't be honest about us at all," says Alonzo.

"They said that the shooter's identity remains in question," continues Louise.

"The police caught the shooter. They have to know who he is," says Ora.

"It's just another Jim Crow game. They'll never press charges against him, because John is Black," insists Alonzo. "Ora, Cleo and Alexia, I should get you home while it's still early. You have a lot to talk about with your grandmothers. They must be very worried about you."

"Thank you, Alonzo. Can we pick up where we left off tomorrow at the office?" asks Ora.

"That's a good idea. Stop by once you've had a chance to calm down," says Alonzo.

"This meal was delicious, Mrs. Willis. Thank you very much for having us," says Cleo.

"It's not often that heroes stop by to see us. You're welcome any time," says Jimmie.

"I'll be here Monday for work," says Alexia.

"That will be fine," says Jimmie to Alexia.

"I'll take your plates," says Louise as she stands up to clean the table.

"Are you ready?" asks Alonzo, looking at Ora.

"Yes, we are," Ora replies.

"Louise, Ora is going to write for us between her studies. She's not going to join the staff just yet, but she'll write when she can," Alonzo says.

"That's good for you, Ora. You're so talented," says Louise.

"I'm hoping to join the staff when you think I'm ready," says Ora.

"It takes time, but if you do a lot more of what you did today, I'll be convinced," says Alonzo.

"Well, try to get some rest," says Louise. Ora, Cleo, Alexia and Alonzo head out toward the car.

"Ora has nine lives like a cat," whispers Jimmie.

"Alonzo's always been afraid to print her letters. They're cryptic," whispers Louise.

Alonzo unlocks and opens the door for Ora and Alexia. Louise waves goodbye to Alonzo. Alonzo walks to the driver's side of the car and unlocks the door for Cleo. They all enter the car. Alonzo drives toward North Miro Street and turns right. He turns left onto Saint Anthony Street.

"That was so nice, Alonzo. We really appreciate the ride home," says Ora.

"It's no problem at all. We're just glad that you're

safe," says Alonzo. He pulls into the front of Ora's house on Annette Street.

Ora, Cleo and Alexia climb out of Alonzo's car onto the curb. They head toward the front door.

"Tell your grandmothers I said hello," says Alonzo as he drives away. They climb the stairs and enter their home.

"We've been worried sick about you. How did you get home through all that confusion?" asks Josephine.

"Alonzo found us at City Hall and gave us a ride home," replies Ora.

"Ora, it's been all over the news that there was a shooting at City Hall," says Ellis.

"We know and we're sorry. We're still really shaken up," says Ora. "We were there when the boy was shot by Walmsley's men."

"Ora, come in and have a seat," says Josephine. They sit down at the kitchen table.

"Would you like some lemonade?" offers Ellis.

Alexia and Cleo shake their heads no. "No thank you, Ma Mum. Alonzo and Louise treated us to lunch at his mother's," replies Ora.

"Well, that's very nice of him," says Ellis.

"Ma Mere and Ma Mum, I have good news," says Ora.

"What is it, sweetie?" asks Josephine.

"Alonzo is interested in me writing for him while I'm in school. He'd like me to write letters and even articles one at a time, so that I can get some experience," answers Ora.

"Well, that is very good news," says Josephine glancing over at Ellis and smiling.

"He will pay me and he'd like to cover all three of us, because we helped to save the boy who was shot today at City Hall," says Ora.

"Oh Ora, we're so proud of you," says Josephine raising her hands in joy.

"You left this morning hoping to become a writer and now you're working for Alonzo. I prayed for you, honey. You really deserve this, Ora," says Ellis.

"So what actually happened today?" asks Josephine.

"We walked all the way to City Hall with the exception of one block," says Ora.

"What happened to the streetcar?" asks Josephine.

"We boarded at Canal, but the seats were filled. A white family got on one block away, so the conductor kicked us off," says Cleo.

"I'm sorry, Cleo," says Ellis.

"We were so rushed and tired, but we made it there just in time," adds Alexia.

"The people pushed us and cursed at us on Canal Street, but we walked right through the crowd," describes Cleo.

"Once we made it to Saint Charles, we knew that we were just in time," says Ora.

"So, how did you get so close to the shooting?" asks Josephine.

"We made it to the Black section off to the side of the stage in front of Gallier Hall. Long's men pulled out their guns when Walmsley's men grabbed the small boy and his parents in the Black section," explains Ora.

"We were directly in front of the scene," says Cleo.

"Did Walmsley's men shoot into the crowd?" asks Josephine.

"Thank heavens no," replies Ora.

"Only one shot was fired and it hit John Smith, Jr. in his leg.

"Praise God. You could have all been seriously injured," says Josephine.

"How could something like this happen at City Hall with so many policemen there?" asks Ellis.

"It's a catastrophe that's been brewing for years between Long and Walmsley. My letter to Alonzo was a warning, but he just wouldn't hear me. Now he's listening carefully," says Ora.

"Ora, it's always been our belief that you should focus on Walmsley's mistreatment of Black people. Now that Alonzo's eyes are open, you can write freely and be published," says Josephine.

"Alonzo still has some questions, but he's slowly understanding the truth," says Cleo.

"Alonzo seems to me to be skeptical," says Alexia. "It's like he can't really believe this all happened."

"Once Alonzo speaks with Dr. Batiste himself, he'll realize that we're telling him the truth about Walmsley's men," says Ora.

"Ora, it's alright to be nervous. This is the beginning of your life as a writer. Even Alonzo's doubts won't stop you now," assures Josephine.

"Alonzo is one of those people who questions Walmsley's hatred of Blacks. He believes that his uptown thinking is too sophisticated to be aligned with lynchers and Jim Crow violence," says Ellis.

"Well, we certainly know better, and it's time to expose Walmsley and his henchmen," says Josephine.

"Ma Mum, I'd like to help you prepare dinner tonight," says Ora. Ellis and Josephine laugh.

"Ora, you're cooking? I can't believe it," says Alexia.

"It's the least I could do for all of you after today," says Ora.

"But aren't you tired, honey?" asks Ellis. "Why don't you get changed up and lay down for a while first."

"Alright, I can change first," says Ora. She and Alexia head over to their room.

"Ora, you're being so sweet. It's not like you at all," teases Alexia.

"I really need to. Today was a disaster," says Ora. She sits down on her bed and removes her shoes. "Ouch. My feet are killing me," she shrieks.

"My whole body is in pain," says Alexia as she sits down on her bed. "How are you going to cook tonight in that condition?" she asks.

Ora chuckles. "If I rest for an hour, I'll make it," she says. Ora stands slowly and shuffles over to her dresser.

She pulls out her nightshirt and shorts. Ora changes her clothes, then returns to her bed and gets under the covers.

"That's it, Ora. Take a short nap," says Alexia. Ora falls soundly asleep.

Alexia turns down the flame in Ora's lantern, and walks out to the kitchen. "She's finally sleeping, Ma Mere," says Alexia.

"Ora has so much work ahead of her. It's good that she's resting," says Josephine.

CHAPTER 3 / "REAL WORK BEGINS"

Alonzo slams down the front page of the *Times Picayune* newspaper on the desk in front of Ora. "Did Long's men draw their guns first, Ora?!" demands Alonzo.

"Yes. I mean no. They reacted to Walmsley's men," responds Ora, shaken by his interrogation.

"Walmsley says this shooting was provoked!" exclaims Alonzo.

"Walmsley's men grabbed and threatened the Smith's and Long's men fought to protect them," responds Ora.

"Ora, this looks terrible for us. We have a shooting that's plain and clear, but it's a political mess," says Alonzo.

"Try to calm down, dear. It's just Walmsley up to his old tricks," consoles Louise.

"I did see Long's men draw their guns, but Walmsley's men may have pulled out their guns first. Long's men definitely didn't shoot anyone," replies Ora.

"You know, that's what really matters. I'm just getting caught up in the headlines and not seeing the story for what it really is," says Alonzo.

"That's right, Alonzo. Let's stay focused," says Louise.

"It all happened so quickly. If you were there, you'd understand that Walmsley's men were a threat to us all. Long's men reacted with the needed force," says Ora.

"Dean Eiffel, a New Orleans man with no prior offenses is the shooter according to the news. Is this the man you recognize from City Hall?" asks Alonzo.

"That's him," replies Ora.

"I'm sorry that I'm so upset. It's just that every time the police are supposed to catch attackers for killing or injuring Black people, they find a reason not to," says Alonzo.

"Dear, you shouldn't demand answers from Ora. We should be speaking directly with Long's men," says Louise.

"Louise, that's an excellent idea. I'll give Senator Long's office a call and try to schedule a meeting," says Alonzo.

"Now that sounds more like the Alonzo I know," says Louise.

"Ora, I'd like you and your father to join us in Baton Rouge when we do meet with Senator Long," says Alonzo.

Ora looks up from her frown over at Louise. "Thank you, Alonzo and Louise. That would be a dream come true," she says.

"Ora, we're definitely still going to feature you, Alexia and Cleo in next week's issue of the paper," assures Alonzo.

"Yes, we're so proud of you," says Louise.

"That's reassuring, because I thought you'd given up on us," says Ora.

"Ora, we'll never give up on you. You've worked so hard. I just can't believe Walmsley's trying to steal this moment from you," responds Alonzo.

"If we don't leave soon, we're going to be late for our visit with the Smith's and Doctor Batiste," says Louise.

"We have thirty minutes," says Alonzo looking down at his watch. "Let's head to Charity now."

Louise picks up her purse and their camera and walks to the front door. Alonzo opens the door for Louise and Ora as the bells chime overhead. They all hop into the car and leave for the hospital. Alonzo turns right from Erato Street where his office is located onto Genois Street. He turns onto the Washington Avenue thoroughfare, then onto Broad Avenue. "The Smith family is really looking forward to seeing you again, Ora. They asked about you and Cleo so much when I called Claude at the hospital this morning," says Alonzo.

"The Smith's handled the shooting with such dignity," says Ora.

"Today should be a very good one despite the finger pointing from Walmsley," says Louise.

"That's for sure. This is the story our readers want to hear, not the gossiping mess that's being reported from Walmsley," says Alonzo. He turns right onto Tulane Avenue toward Charity Hospital. There's heavy traffic, but it doesn't delay them much. "Claude is so impressed with you and Cleo. He was glad to hear that you'll be there."

"I've always admired Doctor Batiste. I'm so glad to

have helped him," says Ora.

"Walmsley's going to be in for a big surprise when he reads the Sepia Socialite and the feature stories on John Smith, Jr. with Doctor Batiste. He's trying to ruin it for us, but the pictures of the Smith's with Doctor Batiste will be worth a thousand words," says Alonzo as he pulls into the parking lot across from the hospital. Alonzo opens the car doors for Louise and Ora. "Let's head into the hospital," he says. They walk toward the separate entrance for Black visitors and enter Charity Hospital. "We're here to visit John Smith, Jr. and Dr. Clause Batiste," says Alonzo.

"Are they expecting you," asks the receptionist.

"Yes, we have an appointment with the Smith family in ten minutes," replies Alonzo.

"Please have a seat. We'll call you in when they're ready," says the receptionist.

Dr. Claude Batiste walks out to the waiting room to greet Alonzo and sees him seated next to Louise and Ora. "Alonzo, you're right on time. Come on back with me," says Doctor Batiste.

"You remember my wife, Louise," says Alonzo.

"Of course. Good morning, Louise and good morning Ora," replies Doctor Batiste. They enter the pediatric intensive care unit for Blacks and walk toward John Smith, Jr.'s room.

"Ora," says Ann Smith when she sees her enter the room. Ann walks over to give Ora a hug.

Ora is pleasantly surprised by the gesture. "Hello, Mrs. Smith. How's John Smith, Jr. doing now?" asks Ora.

"He's doing much better. He's still recovering from his surgery, but they stitched his wounds and administered pain medicine for him," replies Ann.

"Ann, John, John, Jr., I'd like to introduce you to Alonzo Willis and his wife Louise from the Sepia Socialite newspaper," says Doctor Batiste.

"Good morning, Alonzo and Louise," says John Smith, Sr. shaking their hands. "I read your paper often. We're glad that you're here. A lot of papers have called us, but they don't really care much about John, Jr."

"The media is twisting and turning this story in the Jim Crow direction. We're here to really tell your story," assures Alonzo.

"The bullet just missed John, Jr.'s femur. If it had pierced his bone, his leg might have required amputation," explains Doctor Batiste.

"Praise the Lord," says Ann. "The angels and saints

were watching over him and protecting him yesterday."

"Dean Eiffel didn't really get a clean shot. He was reacting to the other men," says John Smith, Sr. "The news is reporting that men drew their guns on Dean first, but we clearly remember seeing and feeling the guns on the men who grabbed us, including Dean. The people standing next to us must have seen Dean's gun too," he continues.

"So you did see guns on the men who grabbed you before the other men drew their guns?" asks Alonzo.

"Absolutely. That's why I shouted to get the attention of the police when they grabbed us. We were defenseless when they attacked us," replies John Smith, Sr.

"Isn't that interesting," says Alonzo.

"We wish we knew the names of the men who fought back," says Ann.

"We know that they're Long's men. Huey P. Long that is," says Alonzo.

"Why would Huey P. Long send his men to Walmsley's speech?" asks Ann.

"They've been fighting for years," replies Alonzo.

"Now I understand why Mayor Walmsley insists on running the story that Dean Eiffel was a victim," says John Smith, Sr.

"Dean Eiffel is one of Walmsley's men. He and the other men are a group of racist killers," says Alonzo.

"We were so blessed to make it out of there alive," says Ann.

"May I take a photograph of the three of you?" asks Louise.

"Sure," replies Ann.

"Could you stand next to John, Jr.'s bed together?" asks Louise pointing to the opposite side of his bed. Ann and John Smith, Sr. walk over to their son's bedside. Ann wraps her arm around John, Jr.'s shoulders and the three of them smile for the picture.

Louise raises the camera and takes the photograph. The flash shines brightly and momentarily fills the shaded room with light. "Let me get one with John, Jr. and Doctor Batiste together with you two," says Louise.

"That's a good one too," says Alonzo.

"You all look so happy together," says Ora. John, Jr. chuckles. Louise takes the second photograph.

"Claude, how soon can John, Jr. be released?" asks Alonzo.

"After surgery, the hospital requires a stay of five days or more," replies Doctor Batiste.

"The good news is that Charity Hospital has offered care to John, Jr. free of charge," says John Smith, Sr.

"Mrs. Smith, we're so glad to hear that the hospital is donating its services to John, Jr." says Louise.

"We're just so relieved by the gift. Emergency care is very expensive," says Ann.

"Yes, and Charity has approved my proposal to practice here at the hospital. The Board has come through with all of the needed support," says Doctor Batiste.

"Congratulations, Claude. I knew they'd see things your way sooner or later," says Alonzo.

"John, Sr. was an orderly for the city before he was let go by Mayor Walmsley," says Ann.

"Now I'm inviting him to join my staff here at Charity," says Doctor Batiste.

"Oh, that's wonderful news," says Louise.

"This has really turned out to be alright after all," says Ann.

"Of course, we're writing several stories about the incident, but we haven't yet decided how to cover your story. What would you like us to write about you?" asks Alonzo.

"It would be really good if you could describe the

shooting from our perspective," responds John Smith, Sr.

"What does this all mean to you?" asks Alonzo.

"Alonzo, the three of us entered City Hall the morning of the speech, so that I could collect my final city check. Unfortunately, I let the city clerks get the best of me. They were rude and they called me names like dirty and poor," explains John Smith, Sr.

"That's horrible," says Louise.

"I asked to speak with someone about being rehired. That's when the clerks pointed me out as disorderly and asked me to leave. When we walked outside, Walmsley's men forced themselves on us. They were openly carrying guns. Dean Eiffel grabbed John, Jr. and I shouted for help from the police. Long's men rushed over to help and one of them pulled out his gun. Dean quickly reacted. He drew his weapon and shot John, Jr. in the leg. We were stunned. Long's men grabbed John, Jr. and captured Dean for the police. Ora and Cleo quickly offered to help us and they found Dr. Batiste. Cleo soon returned with an ambulance. We left for Charity Hospital and we've been here ever since. John, Jr.'s surgery was successful," describes John, Sr.

"That's very helpful, John," says Alonzo.

"I had no idea that Walmsley's men really did threaten you with their guns first," says Ora.

"We saw their guns and we felt them press violently into our backs. Walmsley's men are very dangerous. I'll never try to speak my mind at City Hall again," says John Smith, Sr.

"Daddy, it's not your fault," says John, Jr.

Ann leans in to hug John, Jr. "Oh, that so sweet, son," she says.

"I'm just so glad we were there to help you," says Ora.

"So are we," says Ann. Everyone laughs.

"Well, our work has only begun," says Alonzo. "We're publishing next week's issue with this and several other stories. Then we're heading out to meet with Senator Long himself," he says.

"Now that's a powerful story to tell. We must be pretty special to be in your newspaper," says John Smith, Sr.

"You are very special," says Louise.

"John, Jr. needs to rest," says Doctor Batiste.

"I guess we have everything we need," says Alonzo.

"Thank you for allowing us to visit so soon after the

surgery," says Louise.

"If you can set the story straight and stop the mayhem, we'll be so much better off," says John, Sr.

"Thank you for taking our picture," says John, Jr. Everyone chuckles.

Doctor Batiste leads Alonzo, Louise and Ora out to the hall. "That was really very good," says Doctor Batiste.

"You think so?" asks Alonzo.

"Definitely. They were finally able to tell their side of the story," says Doctor Batiste.

"I'm just worried about what Walmsley will do and say when he reads the story. He'll stop at nothing to get his way," says Alonzo.

"Just be honest and don't be argumentative. Let people know the truth about Dean Eiffel," replies Doctor Batiste.

Alonzo turns to shake Doctor Batiste's hand. "Thank you for everything, Claude. Take good care of the Smith's and congratulations again," says Alonzo. He takes Louise's hand and walks out with her and Ora to the reception area.

"The Smith's are so kind," says Louise.

"Yes they are, but we must make sure to get their

story right. We won't have a second chance," warns Alonzo. He walks Louise and Ora out to the parking lot. Alonzo opens the car doors for them, then climbs in.

"This day has been exciting. I didn't realize that being a writer could be so intense," says Ora.

"This is only the beginning. The more you cover segregation, the more dangerous it becomes," says Louise.

"Your reputation's on the line at all times. People question your every move when you try to fight the system," says Alonzo.

"I'd like to focus on segregation, but the tactics can be so confusing," says Ora.

"Yeah, confusing and risky," says Alonzo. "That's why I'm always so stressed. The expectations are high for our paper. People are watching our every move," he says.

"The Smith story is one of the biggest we've covered so far with a personal aspect. We cover national news, but not local stories this size," says Louise.

"I didn't realize this story was so important to you. Thank goodness, John, Sr. confirmed that Dean threatened him with a gun first," says Ora.

"Yes, Ora, it's very important indeed. When we tell John Smith, Sr.'s real story, the city will be awakened.

We'll have a lot of questions to answer, but the ball will be in our court," says Alonzo.

"That's for sure. Wait 'til Huey P. Long hears about this one," says Louise.

"Long probably knows all about it. He despises the mess made by Walmsley. He watches his every move," says Ora.

Alonzo turns left down Broad Avenue. The traffic is light. He stops at an intersection and notices an elderly woman crossing the opposite street. "She's seen so much more than we ever have," he says.

"That's the truth," says Louise. "She could tell us some stories."

"Ora, you must learn a lot from your grandmothers," says Alonzo. He hits his forehead. "Oh, I forgot that Cleo and Alexia were waiting for us at your house." Alonzo turns around at Howard Avenue back toward Tulane Avenue.

"They haven't been waiting too long. I told them we'd visit the Smith's at Charity first," says Ora.

"I'm so glad you remembered just in time. Cleo and Alexia would have been so disappointed," says Louise.

"My mind is racing a mile a minute. I'm just so glad

John Smith, Sr. cleared everything up for me," says Alonzo. He turns left onto Claiborne Avenue toward Annette Street.

"We'd like to take a photograph of the three of you in front of Corpus Christi," says Louise.

"That's a nice surprise, Louise," says Ora.

"We decided that the setting of the church would capture the spirit of your story," says Alonzo.

"Ma Mere and Ma Mum will be glad to hear that," says Ora.

"The people in the parish will be very proud to see you there," says Alonzo. He pulls up to the front of Ora's home and Cleo and Alexia are outside waiting.

"They're here for us. We'll be back soon," says Alexia to Josephine.

"Be careful out there," says Josephine waving goodbye. Alexia and Cleo walk quickly over to Alonzo's car and climb in.

"Hello, Alexia and Cleo," says Louise. "We're headed to Corpus Christi to photograph you and Ora for the story."

"That's a very nice place for our picture," says Alexia.

"Have you read the news about the shooter being a victim?" asks Cleo.

"We've been fussing and fighting about that lie all morning, Cleo. After meeting with the Smith's everything has been cleared up," replies Alonzo.

"Yeah, don't get him started, Cleo. He's finally calm now," says Louise.

"Cleo, the shooter, Dean Eiffel, and Walmsley's men are killers who openly threatened the Smith's with their guns before the shooting," says Ora.

"I'm so confused now. I thought Long's men drew their guns first," says Alexia.

"We didn't see everything. We missed the first few seconds," replies Ora.

"Well, that's very good news. I was beginning to wonder if we'd lost the story," says Alexia.

Alonzo turns onto Saint Bernard Avenue and parks at the curb in front of Corpus Christi Church. The church is simply beautiful and the parish is very supportive of Ora's family. Alonzo walks over to open the car doors for Louise, Ora and Alexia. They walk to the front steps of the church.

"Ora, stand in the middle. Cleo, stand on her left and Alexia, stand on her right," says Louise motioning with her free hand. "That's it. Come in a little closer. You're right at the center of the church doors," says Louise. She snaps the picture and the flash shines brightly. "Let me take a second shot just in case we need it. Cleo, stand in the center this time with Ora and Alexia on either side." Cleo moves to the center and Ora moves to Cleo's side.

Ora pinches Cleo's hand whispering, "We're celebrities now."

"You started this," whispers Cleo. They smile brightly for the camera.

"That's it," says Louise. "The Smith's are going to really like this one."

"Everyone will like it except Walmsley and his flock," says Alonzo.

"Well, that's it for us. We'll head back to your house unless you need a ride somewhere else, Cleo and Alexia," says Louise.

"No, that's all we expected for today," says Cleo.

Alonzo opens his car doors for Louise, Ora and Alexia. They all climb into the car. Alonzo turns onto Claiborne Avenue from Saint Bernard Avenue. "Our story on the three of you will highlight your heroic deeds," he says.

"It should be very nice," says Alexia.

"I'll write the article, but Ora will write the story first," says Alonzo.

"That will help to keep us in line," says Louise. Everyone laughs.

Alonzo pulls into the front of Ora's home. "Ora's staying for the ride back to our office," he says.

"Well, thanks again for featuring us and for the pictures," says Alexia.

"Yeah, they were a pleasant surprise," says Cleo. Alexia and Cleo hop out of the car and walk to their front door.

Josephine is waiting there for them. "That didn't take very long," she says.

"They surprised us and drove us to Corpus Christi for the photos," replies Alexia.

"Oh, how wonderful. Alonzo certainly is a nice young man," says Josephine.

"Alonzo is changing Ora's life," says Ellis.

Alonzo turns right onto Claiborne Avenue toward Tulane Avenue.

"We have the photographs of the three heroes and the photos of the Smith's with Claude. Now we need photographs of the factual scene of the shooting," says Louise.

"Louise, you're right. I'll take Poydras Street ahead before we return to the office," says Alonzo.

"Ora, we'd like to photograph you at City Hall for the story," says Louise.

"That's unexpected," says Ora.

"It's a good representation of the events that occurred yesterday for you to be there," says Louise. Alonzo turns left onto Poydras Street and right onto Camp Street to park. Alonzo opens the passenger side doors for Louise and Ora.

"Ora, can you stand where the incident began with the Smith's?" asks Louise. Blood stains cover the street despite the obvious cleaning. Ora reflects back to the trauma of the day.

"Ora, if you're still a little shaken, we can wait," says Alonzo.

"I'm a little upset about Walmsley, that's all," says Ora straightening up for the camera.

"It's a lot to think about," says Louise. Ora smiles and stands up tall. "Are you ready?" asks Louise.

"I'm ready," says Ora.

"That's lovely. Now how would you like to take one directly in front of Gallier Hall?" asks Louise.

"Now that would be great," says Ora walking over to the front steps of Gallier Hall.

Louise raises her camera, "Move over a little to the left. Now that's it. Smile," directs Louise. Ora smiles and the second flash makes Ora a little dizzy. Louise walks over to Ora and gives her a hug. "You've made it through the chaos. You must be eager to get back to the office and begin writing," she says.

"I have a lot on my mind and writing is my only way out," says Ora.

"Ladies, let's get going before Walmsley sees us here and harasses us," says Alonzo. Louise and Ora follow Alonzo to his car. They climb in and leave quickly. Alonzo turns down Poydras Street toward Loyola Avenue.

"I didn't realize how different it would be to return to City Hall and the scene so soon," says Ora.

"These things take time. You've been through so much in such a short period that your mind hasn't healed," says Louise.

Alonzo turns left onto Tulane Avenue toward Broad Avenue. "Ora, they'll be many incidents like this one that you'll cover as a writer. You have to be prepared for the worst," says Alonzo.

"This one was special. She experienced something more than mere coverage of a story. She helped to save a life," says Louise.

"Ora has the potential to save many lives with her writing and leadership. Our job is to bring it out of her and give the people something they've never seen before from a young Black woman," says Alonzo. He turns left onto Erato Street, then parks in the driveway of his office. Alonzo opens the passenger side doors of his car for Louise and Ora. Alonzo opens the office front door for the women to enter. The bells chime overhead. Ora takes a seat at a desk. Alonzo and Louise organize their camera and notes. Alonzo walks over to Ora and asks, "Are you ready?"

"I'm ready to begin," replies Ora. "My article on Mayor Walmsley will expose the extreme violence and hatred perpetuated by the men who closely follow him from the White League."

"That's the article we need, but I'm not sure if we're ready for it just yet," says Alonzo.

"We can't censor Ora's writing. She must have the freedom to write what's essential and relevant to our readers," says Louise.

"You know better than I do that Ora writes very scathing critiques of Mayor Walmsley," says Alonzo.

"I'm not afraid to openly criticize Mayor Walmsley," says Ora.

"You're not afraid yet, but you haven't faced off with Mayor Walmsley yet. Once you confront him in the press, he'll attack you just as he's done so many opponents," says Alonzo.

"That's a risk I'm willing to take," replies Ora.

"Ora, you can subtly critique Walmsley without risking your safety," says Louise.

"There's just no way around Walmsley. Huey P. Long can't stop him. We can't expose him. He twists and tampers with the news," says Ora.

"Ora, your frustration is a reflection of your conscientious thoughts," says Alonzo.

"Ora, you're right about Walmsley. We just need to channel your frustration into clever friendly fire that doesn't enrage Walmsley," says Louise.

"He'll be angry just to see positive pictures of Ora, Cleo and Alexia celebrating John, Jr.'s recovery. Whether she writes a critique or not, we'll have to deal with

Walmsley's backlash," says Alonzo.

"Do you think that Walmsley already knows who I am?" asks Ora.

"There's a very real possibility," replies Alonzo. Walmsley lives and breathes for these moments. He has his men hunt down information on everyone involved in every racial incident," says Alonzo.

"Let's give him something to think about," says Ora.

"Ora is right. If Walmsley already knows everything about us, we should directly address him and the racist violence they experience," says Louise.

"I'll give this some thought," says Alonzo. "Let's focus on the stories about the Smith family and Claude."

"I'll develop the photographs," says Louise as she takes the camera into the darkroom.

"I'm eager to see today's pictures," says Alonzo.

"She took some great shots today. Everyone will be so glad to see them," says Ora.

"Ora, do you think that Walmsley will have Dean Eiffel released by the police?" asks Alonzo.

"He's capable of just about anything. I wouldn't put it past him," says Ora.

"Ora, listen to this story in the *Times Picayune* on

Walmsley. 'Mayor Walmsley witnessed an attack by a group of armed men on Dean Eiffel. The men threatened Eiffel with pistols and grabbed him forcefully. Eiffel fired his weapon in self-defense, accidentally hitting a Negro boy. Eiffel was arrested by police. Mayor Walmsley safely left the City Hall stage.' Walmsley is really pouring it on thick," says Alonzo.

"Mayor Walmsley is using the typical Jim Crow manipulation tactics to deflect the blame and guilt. He's a classic racist politician with an ulterior motive," says Ora.

"You're right. We have to get rid of Walmsley somehow, but he's just so slick. When we meet with Senator Long, we can devise a strategy to put pressure on Walmsley," says Alonzo.

"Before the shooting, my plan was to gather information on Walmsley's attacks on Blacks and report it directly to Senator Long. Your approach is definitely better, Alonzo," says Ora.

"So, instead of printing an article that openly criticizes Walmsley, we can plan something bigger with Long. We can work with Long to get rid of Walmsley," says Alonzo.

"I never imagined that I would come this close to

Mayor Walmsley and Senator Long. I study them both so much, and now they know who I am. It's unbelievable," says Ora.

"Soon you'll actually meet with Senator Long. Are you really prepared to hear what he has to say?" asks Alonzo.

"I'm not ready yet, but I'm hoping to work with you to prepare," replies Ora.

"Long will expect you to know the ins and outs of New Orleans politics, everything about Walmsley there is to know," says Alonzo.

"I'll be ready for Long. I won't let you down, Alonzo," assures Ora.

"If you write the story on you, Cleo and Alexia, you can begin writing a fairly neutral story on Mayor Walmsley that refutes his description of Dean Eiffel's attack," says Alonzo.

"That would be great. I'll get to work on the two stories now," says Ora. Louise emerges from the darkroom.

"The photographs will be ready in a few hours," she says.

"Louise we were discussing a possible article on Walmsley," says Alonzo.

"That's a good thing," says Louise.

"I'd like Ora to write the truth about the shooting and about Walmsley, not just a critique," says Alonzo.

"The truth is a critique of Walmsley," says Louise. Everyone laughs.

"Louise, we have a lot of work to do this coming week. Ora will need to be here each day with us," says Alonzo.

"I'm definitely looking forward to having Ora here with us from now on," says Louise.

"I'm glad to be here. I've hoped to write for you for so long and now I have a lot to write about," says Ora.

"We should have done this sooner. We're lucky that you're still available," says Louise.

"I might have gotten a few calls from the *Times Picayune* and the *New Orleans Item*, but I turned them down instead," laughs Ora.

"It's funny, but it could be true, considering everything that's happened," says Alonzo.

"They will begin to call you one day soon, Ora. Just work hard and write from your heart," says Louise.

"When your writing is strong enough, I'll certainly recommend you for positions with any major paper in the state," says Alonzo.

"I have a long way to go," says Ora.

"I'm just hoping you'll get used to being published. When you have strong topics, we'll always look to you for great stories," says Louise.

"The key is to take it one step at a time. Now that Walmsley knows who you are, he'll be watching your every move," says Alonzo.

"When you write honestly, the people will listen to what you have to say. Even Walmsley will have a hard time convincing people that you're wrong about anything," says Louise.

"Right now, people are listening closely to you," says Alonzo. "The shooting has them on edge and upset about racism. You represent what's good and right about our city."

"I want to make a difference for people who are suffering in silence," says Ora.

"You can and you will. Just stay focused and write about the things that matter to you most," says Alonzo.

"How many people do you think know about me already?" asks Ora.

"Word travels quickly. A good number of people

have heard about you and Cleo, but many more will know when we release the paper," replies Alonzo.

"Ora, this is the perfect way to start your writing career. Everyone will look for your next articles and letters from now on, because of what you've done," says Louise.

"If you'd begun earlier, it might have been too soon. Our timing is perfect," adds Alonzo.

"I'm a little nervous and it's difficult for me to focus with everything in mind," says Ora.

"Try to calm down. We won't let you fail. Just write what comes to mind and we'll help you to make sense of it all," says Louise.

"We know that your first thoughts won't be perfect, but it's our job to develop your writing skills, especially now that the community looks to you for the truth," says Alonzo.

"It's very important to me that I do well. Everything I study and think about involves writing and bringing an end to segregation. I just don't want to let the people down," says Ora.

"Ora, you sound a lot like me when I was your age. You just have much more talent and heart," says Alonzo.

"I didn't realize you felt that way about my writing.

I always assumed that you considered me an awkward novice," says Ora.

"Certainly not, Ora. I have been concerned about risks that you were willing to take," says Alonzo.

"Alonzo thought that you were too young to confront Mayor Walmsley in the press. Now that you're in the public eye, you have the freedom to write about segregation like a seasoned journalist," says Louise.

"I'll follow your lead, Louise and Alonzo. This is the defining moment of my life," says Ora.

"We're glad to be here at this turning point for you," says Louise.

"Without the two of you, I would have been lost in the crowd of hopefuls, waiting for a change that would have never come," says Ora.

"Well, you certainly have our attention now," says Alonzo.

"When you speak, we listen, Ora. Your words and actions are invaluable," says Louise.

"Ora, the desk where you're sitting will be your space from now on. When you're here, you can work there and write," says Alonzo.

"Thank you, Alonzo," replies Ora.

"Monday I will call Huey P. Long's office to request a meeting. Once they confirm, you can call your father to invite him to join us in Baton Rouge," says Alonzo.

"He's going to be so surprised to hear that we're meeting with Huey P. Long," says Ora.

"Have you spoken with him yet about what you did for the Smith's?" asks Alonzo.

"I haven't had a moment to myself. I'll give him a call tomorrow afternoon," replies Ora.

"He's going to be very proud of you, Ora. We'll have to mail copies of the paper to him once it's printed with your pictures. I can't wait to hear his reaction," says Alonzo.

"My father encouraged me to write for you for over a year. He's eagerly awaited this kind of news from me, Alonzo and Louise," says Ora.

"Having you here is like having your father with us all over again," says Alonzo.

"I wish he was actually here with us, but I'm older now and I'm able to deal with his absence," says Ora.

"It's a part of growing up. The harder you work, the more independent you become," says Louise.

"Well, let's take a look at the story on the Smith's

and Claude," says Alonzo.

"I'll begin by writing what I witnessed and what the Smith's shared, then having you review it," says Ora.

"That sounds good. I'll get started on the story about you and Cleo," says Alonzo.

"I'd like to write something on Walmsley that could help Ora to focus her thoughts. Would that be alright with you, Alonzo?" asks Louise.

"Yes, that would be good for Ora," replies Alonzo. Ora, Louise and Alonzo begin to write their stories. They review the coverage in the *Times Picayune* and the *New Orleans Item*. They write, rewrite and edit their stories.

Ora walks over to Alonzo with her rough draft and asks, "Would you like to take a look at what I've written so far?"

"Of course, Ora. Let me see what you have," replies Alonzo. Ora hands her papers to Alonzo. He reads the first few lines. "John Smith, Sr., Ann Smith and their son visited City Hall on Friday, August 2, 1935. As they walked outside to hear Mayor Thomas Semmes Walmsley's speech, they were attacked by Dean Eiffel. Eiffel threatened the Smith family with a gun. John Smith, Sr. called for help, then Eiffel shot his son in his left leg. Police apprehended Eiffel as the crowd ran away in fear."

"Ora, that's pretty good writing for your first try," says Louise.

"We can work on it together this week. Ora, let's get you home in time for dinner," says Alonzo.

"We were just getting started," says Ora.

"You've been through so much in the last two days. Take a break and come back on Monday," says Louise. Ora walks to the front door. Alonzo opens the door for Ora and Louise as the bells chime overhead. He unlocks and opens his car door for them. They climb into his car.

"I'm really looking forward to next week," says Ora.

"We are too, Ora. It will be one of the biggest weeks for the paper this year, because of the news," says Louise. Alonzo turns onto Washington Avenue toward South Carrollton Avenue.

"I still can't believe this happened yesterday. It's surreal," says Ora.

"Imagine how we felt when we realized that it was you who saved John Smith, Jr.'s life. You definitely surprised us, Ora," says Louise.

"When I heard about you, Cleo and Alexia at City Hall, I knew it had to be you who everyone was clamoring about," says Alonzo as he turns right onto Tulane Avenue.

"Everything happened so quickly that I wasn't really aware of any attention," says Ora.

"A lot of people witnessed your heroics. We're very proud of you, Ora," says Alonzo.

"I don't know if it will ever happen again," says Ora.

"Ora, you don't have to ever do it again. Once is enough for a lifetime," says Louise. Ora smiles. Alonzo turns left onto Claiborne Avenue toward Annette Street.

"Ora, tell your father that I said hello and congratulations," says Alonzo.

"I will," says Ora.

"Let's plan a get together next Sunday with your grandmothers. I've been putting it off for too long," says Alonzo.

"That would be really nice," replies Ora. Alonzo pulls up to Ora's house on Annette Street. "Thanks again Alonzo and Louise," says Ora.

"Thank you, Ora. We really appreciate having you with us," says Alonzo. "Tell your grandmothers I said good evening."

"I will," says Ora as she walks to her front door and

waves goodbye. As Ora opens her front door, she smells a delicious meal waiting for her on the kitchen table.

"Ora, you're back just in time for dinner," says Ellis.

"Come on in and get cleaned up," says Josephine.

"Hello, Ma Mere and Ma Mum. I'm glad to be home," says Ora. "Has Papa called?"

"Not yet, sweetie," replies Josephine.

"Alonzo reminded me to call him and tell him about what happened yesterday," says Ora.

"Alonzo must be pretty excited about what you've done," says Josephine.

"Yes, he is. He's even invited me to meet with Huey P. Long in Baton Rouge with Papa," says Ora.

"Ora, he didn't? I can't believe what I'm hearing. Today was a very big day for you indeed," says Josephine.

"Well, come on in and get ready for dinner. We have a lot to talk about with you tonight," says Ellis. Ora walks through the kitchen and the hallway into her bedroom. Alexia is in the room sewing a blouse for work.

"Hey there, Ora. How was it?" asks Alexia.

"I survived the day, but I'm beat," replies Ora.

"I knew that today was tough for you. You seemed really tense when you picked us up for the pictures," says

Alexia.

Ora changes into a casual shirt and shorts. "I'll tell you the whole story when you come out to the kitchen for dinner," Ora says.

"I'm coming. I just need a few minutes to finish up this blouse for Mrs. Willis," Alexia says as Ora walks out to the kitchen. Alexia places the blouse down on her bed, then jumps up to follow Ora. Cleo is sitting at the kitchen table.

"So, how was your day?" asks Cleo.

"It was tough, but I'm so happy now, Cleo. Thank you for everything," replies Ora.

"So, tell us about your meeting with Huey P. Long," says Josephine.

"Meeting with Huey P. Long?" asks Alexia.

"The U.S. Senator?" asks Cleo.

"Yes, Cleo and Alexia. Alonzo invited me to meet with him, Louise, Papa and U.S. Senator Huey P. Long at his office in Baton Rouge about Mayor Walmsley," replies Ora.

"That's unbelievable," says Alexia.

"Congratulations, Ora," says Cleo.

"The day didn't begin so well. Alonzo was very

upset about the coverage of Dean Eiffel as a victim. He snapped at me and he interrogated me this morning," says Ora.

"Ora, I know it's a tough job, but if you can hang in there, it's no telling what you can do," says Josephine.

"So whose idea was it for you to take the pictures at Corpus Christi?" asks Josephine.

"It was Alonzo's idea. He really calmed down a lot when we met with the Smith family at Charity. They explained the gun threats by Dean Eiffel that set off the shooting," says Ora.

"Dean Eiffel threatened the Smith's with his gun before Long's men?" asks Cleo.

"Yes, Cleo. Dean Eiffel and the group of Walmsley's men threatened the Smith's with their guns first," replies Ora.

"Isn't that something? Walmsley's up to his old tricks again, telling lies and confusing everyone," says Ellis.

"Ma Mum, Walmsley completely changed the story and gave the impression that Dean Eiffel was forced to act in self-defense when he shot little John, Jr." says Ora.

"Ora, I understand. Mayor Walmsley will do

anything to defend racism," says Ellis.

"Almost anything. He hasn't killed anyone yet," says Josephine.

"I wouldn't put it past him," says Ellis.

"So what's for dinner?" asks Cleo.

"We're having jambalaya and black beans tonight," replies Ellis.

Josephine begins to serve the food. "You should call your father tonight and not wait until tomorrow," suggests Josephine.

"I will," says Ora remorsefully.

"You don't want him to find out about the shooting the hard way," says Josephine.

"No I don't. I'll call him right after dinner," says Ora.

"So, what are they writing about us, Ora?" asks Cleo.

"They've actually invited me to write the stories, so that they can hear our perspective," replies Ora. Cleo and Alexia enjoy the meal. Ora takes a small serving of jambalaya and black beans.

"Would you like some lemonade?" offers Josephine.

"Yes, thank you," replies Ora.

Josephine and Ellis sit down to eat. "This is pretty good. No wonder it's so quiet in here," Josephine says. Everyone laughs.

"I appreciate everything you've done. I never could have done any of this without you," says Ora.

"That's alright, Ora. You've done it and now there's no turning back," says Alexia.

"I feel like a new person," says Ora.

"You are a new person. You have a new purpose," says Josephine.

"You're not hoping and dreaming of making a difference anymore," says Ellis.

"I'm proud to have you as a sister," says Alexia.

"We all did what we knew was right and what you've taught us, Ma Mere and Ma Mum," says Cleo.

"Cleo, there's a little bit more to it," says Josephine. "When Mayor Walmsley's involved, his reputation and segregation is on the line."

"You have to realize that any kind of challenge to Walmsley's authority is a threat. No matter how good you are, he just won't tolerate it," adds Ellis. They finish their dinner.

"I'll take those plates," says Josephine.

"I'm going to give Papa a call," says Ora as she walks over to the phone.

"Break the news to him gently," says Josephine.

"I will, Ma Mere. He hasn't heard from me in a while, so I have a lot to explain," says Ora. Ora picks up the phone and dials her father's number.

The phone rings and Nathan Lewis answers, "Good evening. Who's there?"

"It's Ora," she replies.

"How have you been?" asks Nathan.

"I have a lot of good news for you, Papa," replies Ora.

"What's happening? Are you writing for Alonzo yet?" Nathan asks.

"Papa, Alonzo has offered me a part-time writing opportunity, because Cleo and I saved the life of a boy who was shot at City Hall yesterday," replies Ora.

"Ora, I'm very concerned about you now. How were you and Cleo involved?" he asks.

"We witnessed the shooting by Walmsley's men of a small Black boy just before the mayor's speech," replies Ora. "I provided a doctor and Cleo provided the ambulance," she explains.

"Are you in any danger?" asks Nathan.

"No, everything is fine now, Papa. Alonzo has invited you and me to meet with him and Senator Huey P. Long in Baton Rouge," Ora says.

"Huey P. Long? Alonzo wants you to work at that level already?" asks Nathan.

"Yes, he's ready for me to be a journalist," replies Ora.

"Isn't that something? My girl Ora has finally done it. Congratulations!" says Nathan.

"So will you join us at the meeting, Papa?" asks Ora.

"Of course I will. I wouldn't miss it for the world. Just let me know the date and time," replies Nathan.

"Alonzo's printing several stories about the incident including one on Cleo and me. We will mail this coming issue of the Sepia Socialite to you with our pictures," Ora says.

"That would be wonderful. I'm really looking forward to seeing you again soon, Ora," says Nathan.

"I'll be so glad to see you as well, Papa," says Ora.

"Well, get some rest and call me with the details on

Baton Rouge," says Nathan.

"I will, Papa. Goodnight," says Ora.

"Goodnight to you, Cleo and Alexia," Nathan says. Ora gently hangs up the phone.

"So what was his reaction?" asks Josephine.

"He was very worried about us and the shooting," replies Ora.

"I knew he would be concerned. Your father will want to know everything about Walmsley and the shooting," says Josephine.

"I will give him a call back in a few days once Alonzo's confirmed the date for the Long meeting," says Ora.

"Ora it's been a long couple of days. Why don't you go get some rest?" Ellis says.

"You're right, Ma Mum. I'll go get some sleep now," says Ora as she walks down the hall to her bedroom. Ora changes into her robe, then heads to the bathroom to clean up. Alexia enters their bedroom and begins to work on her blouse again. Ora finishes up in the bathroom, then returns to their bedroom to change into her night gown.

"You ready for bed?" asks Alexia.

"Yes, it's been a long day," replies Ora.

"Well, I won't bother you," says Alexia. Ora turns down the flame in her lantern and snuggles under her covers. "I can finish this blouse in the living room," says Alexia as she heads out to the hallway. Ora falls asleep peacefully.

CHAPTER 4 / "MEETING LONG"

Ora jumps out of bed. She runs to her closet to get dressed. Alexia is startled. She turns over in her bed. "What time is it, Ora?" she asks.

"It's five forty-five," replies Ora. "Today's the big day."

"I'm going back to sleep for fifteen minutes," Alexia says.

Ora dashes out to the hallway and into the bathroom. She brushes her teeth and combs her hair in the mirror. She changes into her dress. "Yes!" she exclaims, pumping her fist. Ora walks back to her room to grab her purse. She flips the cover over Alexia's head. "Wake up, little sister."

"Goodbye," says Alexia with a smile.

"You're going to miss breakfast," says Ora.

"Just go enjoy your day and leave me be," replies Alexia.

Ora laughs, then makes her way out to the kitchen. "Good morning, Ma Mere and Ma Mum."

"Good morning, Ora. You're up early today. You must be excited," says Josephine.

"You know I'm ready for the day. I still can't believe that I'm actually going to meet Huey P. Long," says Ora.

"It's really happening for you, Ora. I'm so excited about last week's issue of the Sepia Socialite. The articles and pictures were so beautiful," says Josephine.

"I'm just so proud of you and Cleo," says Ellis.

"Walmsley must be very upset to see your articles. Let's hope he doesn't lash out at you," says Josephine.

"Have you seen the front page of the *Times Picayune* this morning? Walmsley must be having a fit. Huey P. Long is the center of attention," says Ellis.

"What's happening? Let me see today's paper," says Ora.

"The papers are covering Long as a candidate for president. Here, take a look," says Josephine handing the newspaper to Ora.

"This is big news. Long will be really glad to see it today," says Ora.

"Long's Share Our Wealth plan is the answer to the troubles of the Great Depression. Even FDR has borrowed his ideas to steady the colliding waves of the economy," Josephine says.

"Long is already a winner in my eyes," Ora says.

"Would you like eggs, bacon and toast with orange juice?" offers Ellis.

"That would be great," replies Ora. Ellis serves Ora's breakfast.

"Ora, are you ready for Long? He might want to discuss his policies with you. What are you going to say?" asks Josephine.

"I've studied Long so much that it comes naturally. I'll be a little nervous, but I'll try to do my best," replies Ora.

"You know I'll be praying for you to do well," says

Ellis.

"I'll be praying too," adds Josephine.

Ora enjoys her breakfast. She thinks about her grandmothers and how much they'd encouraged her to be a journalist. She realizes that the day is very important to them and their dreams for her. "I won't let you down, Ma Mere and Ma Mum," she says.

"You could never let us down as hard as you work, Ora," replies Josephine.

"Your faith in me is such a blessing. I will fight for desegregation as long as I live and become the leader that you know I can be," says Ora.

"Now that's what we want to hear from you, Ora. Hold on to that purpose," says Ellis.

"Meeting with Long makes me realize that anything is possible," Ora says.

"We knew that you could do it, Ora. You just had to believe in yourself," says Ellis.

"I'll never forget this day and how much you've encouraged me, Ma Mere and Ma Mum," Ora says. She finishes her breakfast and Ellis clears the table. "I'll go wait at the front door for Alonzo," says Ora as she walks to the living room.

"He should be here in a few minutes," says Ellis.

"We're having lunch at Papa's, so you don't need to pack a lunch for me today," Ora says.

"That should be nice. Tell Ida and the girls that we said hello," says Josephine.

Ora opens the front door and she sees Alonzo and Louise outside waiting for her. Ora turns to her grandmothers and says, "Alonzo's here. I'll be back this afternoon."

"Be careful on your journey today," says Josephine.

Ora walks out to Alonzo's car and opens the door. "Good morning, Alonzo and Louise. How are you today?" asks Ora.

"Good morning, Ora. We're great. It's good to see you," says Louise.

"Hi there, Ora. Let's head out to Baton Rouge," says Alonzo.

Ora closes her car door and gets comfortable. "Have you seen the front page coverage of Huey P. Long's bid for the presidency?" asks Ora.

"Of course we have. It's all over the news. They're projecting that he'd win Louisiana," says Louise.

"Huey P. Long is very serious about competing with

Roosevelt. He has the charisma and the platform to win. He just needs to survive the attacks from his opponents," says Alonzo.

"I can't wait to see Long run for president. Louisiana would be transformed," Ora says.

"Louisiana and America. There's no one like Huey P. Long," says Louise.

Alonzo drives down Claiborne Avenue toward the River Road, because there is heavy construction on Airline Highway. "I met Long for the first time in 1930 during his campaign for the United States Senate. I volunteered for his campaign. I was a freelance journalist, but I hadn't yet launched my paper," explains Alonzo. He turns onto the River Road toward Metairie and Baton Rouge.

"You've known Long for nearly five years?" inquires Ora.

"Yes, he introduced himself to me days before he was elected. It came as a big surprise," replies Alonzo.

"How did he come to notice you?" asks Ora.

"He said that I was one of the most dedicated volunteers in his campaign. He really appreciated me, because I was likely denied the right to vote and I still worked so hard," replies Alonzo.

"So, you've been a Long supporter for years. He knows you pretty well?" asks Ora.

"Yes, I've tried to keep in touch with him, letting him know about the paper and mailing copies of key issues to him. It's been a really good experience for me," replies Alonzo.

"Alonzo is actually very modest about his friendship with Long. If there's ever been anything he needed, Long has always delivered," says Louise.

"That's the kind of friend I need," says Ora. Alonzo drives past Destrehan Plantation. Ora notices the Greek Revival Doric columns of the historic site. She's seen the plantation many times before, but this time she questions slavery.

"Have you ever visited Destrehan Plantation," asks Louise.

"Of course not. I don't get wrapped up in the mystique of the architecture," replies Ora.

"The plantations remind me of Jim Crow. I'll be glad to say goodbye to the River Road when Long completes construction of Airline Highway," says Louise.

"So will I, Louise. I visit my dad in Baton Rouge pretty often and we're so tired of seeing the many plantations along the way. Long is a genius to have thought of Airline Highway," says Ora.

"Long is a genius. He seems to think of everything, even at the federal level. That's why Roosevelt is not quite sure of how to stop him," says Louise.

Alonzo drives through Edgard past San Francisco Plantation. He says, "There's some interesting lessons to be learned in the plantation homes. We shouldn't just ignore the history."

"San Francisco Plantation is an ornate steamboat Gothic. The slaves who suffered never enjoyed the flamboyance," says Louise.

"San Francisco Planation was originally owned by Elisée Rillieux, a free person of color. Unfortunately, the lucrative sale of the plantation to Edmond Marmillion led to dire hardship of the slaves," says Alonzo.

"That's very interesting. I didn't realize that San Francisco Plantation had a Black owner at one time," says Louise.

"My father often tells me stories of Black masters. Some of the stories are interesting, but emancipation is most fascinating," Ora says.

"You're right, Ora. I've studied slavery a lot. I hope

to live to see desegregation," says Alonzo. He drives past the Judge Felix Poche Plantation and Ora doesn't notice it.

"Ora, let's focus on today's meeting. There's nothing that you need to say in particular to Long. Just introduce yourself and let him do the talking," says Louise.

"Yes, Long is very talkative. He'll want to discuss Walmsley and what he's heard about the shooting," says Alonzo.

"Long's men have probably told him the truth about the shooting," says Ora.

"Long spoke with me about Walmsley. He's very concerned about his reaction to the shooting. The lies that he's told to the press in defense of Dean Eiffel are very offensive to Long," says Alonzo.

"Do you think that Long's men have mentioned me to him?" asks Ora.

"I'm more than sure that they have," replies Alonzo. "When he finally sees last week's issue of the paper today, he'll be glad to see your stories."

"I really hope so. I just want to make a good impression on Long, not just today, but for the bright future ahead," says Ora.

"You will make a good impression, Ora. Just

remember that we're here for you no matter what happens today with Long. We need you and we're proud to have you," says Louise.

Alonzo drives through St. Gabriel within minutes of Baton Rouge. The communities along the River Road are polarized and segregated. There is little development beyond the agricultural expanse. Many of the people rely on the bustling Baton Rouge economy for their sustenance and supplies. Long connects with the people who live in these small communities despite his liberal stance on equality. Long frequents the towns between Baton Rouge and New Orleans to maintain his sense of hands-on leadership. Alonzo and Louise are not afraid to travel throughout these connected parishes and they often visit Baton Rouge to cover activity in the capitol city. "We're almost there, Ora. Remind me to bring the papers in to Long. He's waiting to see the Walmsley coverage," says Alonzo.

"I will remind you when we're there. What time is it now?" asks Ora.

"It's twenty minutes to eight," says Alonzo looking down at his watch.

"We should make it there just in time for our nine

o'clock meeting. If we're late at all, Long will have to cancel our meeting," says Louise.

"Don't worry, Louise. We'll be fine," says Alonzo as he zooms down the River Road.

"My dad must be waiting for us at the capitol building now," says Ora.

"I look forward to seeing him there," Alonzo says.

"He could have given me a ride to Baton Rouge this weekend, but I would have missed working with you yesterday," says Ora.

"It was better for you to wait and ride with us. It didn't take any extra time and we wanted to make sure that you arrived," says Louise.

"So what does your father have in mind to say to Long?" asks Alonzo.

"He doesn't really have an agenda. He's just looking forward to meeting Long for the first time," replies Ora.

"If I know Nathan, he has a few things on his mind to say, but he might wait to put them in writing instead," says Alonzo.

"Yes, Papa is known for writing very pointed letters and articles," says Ora.

"He's really just coming to be supportive of Ora this

time, Alonzo. He's probably very proud of her," Louise says.

"My dad is cautiously optimistic about Long. He believes in his message, but he's waiting for him to deliver on segregation," explains Ora.

"That's a good way of thinking about him. At times, I feel the same way," says Louise.

"Long has worked for equity in voting and the economy. He openly fights white supremacists. He's so far ahead of his time. Even Roosevelt could learn a thing or two from Long," says Alonzo.

"If Long were president, he'd bring an end to Jim Crow segregation," says Ora.

"That's what we're all hoping. It'll take everything he's got and much more to win the White House," says Alonzo. He approaches Baton Rouge. The traffic is heavy and the drivers are frenzied as he moves closer to the capitol.

"We should be a little early," says Louise.

"It's eight thirty now," Alonzo says. He enters the state capitol building parking lot.

"Who are you here to see?" asks the security guard.

"We have an appointment with Senator Long,"

responds Alonzo.

"What is your name?" asks the security guard.

"My name is Alonzo Willis," he replies.

The security guard checks his log for Alonzo's name. "I see you here. Come on in," he says as he lifts the parking barrier gate.

"Thank you," says Alonzo. He drives into the parking lot section reserved for Blacks and finds a spot.

"I see my father there," says Ora. Nathan is waiting in his car for Ora, Alonzo and Louise. Alonzo parks his car next to Nathan. "Papa, good morning," Ora says.

"Good morning. You made it here just in time," says Nathan as he embraces Ora.

"Did you have trouble with the security guard?" asks Alonzo.

"No, I gave them my Southern University ID," replies Nathan.

"I gave Long's office your name," says Alonzo.

"They must have also seen my name on his schedule," Nathan says.

"Well the good thing is that we're all here early. Let's head inside and get situated for the meeting," says Alonzo. Louise, Ora and Nathan follow Alonzo into the building. The massive complex is the tallest capitol structure in the United States and it was constructed by Huey P. Long in 1932. It's relatively quiet inside and the level of security is high. There are a handful of visitors walking through the halls. Alonzo walks directly to Governor Oscar K. Allen's office that Long shares. He remembers to bring the Sepia Socialite newspapers with him. "Where's my reminder about the newspapers?" teases Alonzo.

"I forgot. I'm sorry," says Ora. The four of them enter the waiting area of Governor Allen's office.

"Good morning. We're here for our nine o'clock meeting with Senator Long," says Alonzo.

"Good morning, Alonzo. Everyone can have a seat over there. I'll let Senator Long know that you're here," says Margaret Wright, the governor's secretary.

"Thank you, Margaret," says Alonzo as they all take a seat.

Suddenly, a man pulls the door to the office open from the hallway. He shouts, "Impeach Huey P. Long! Impeach him now!" Long's armed bodyguard state police grab the man. The guards arrest him and remove him from the state capitol building. The state police secure the area surrounding Governor Allen's office. They enter the office and closely monitor everyone inside.

"I can't believe he did that," says Louise. Ora sits quietly, afraid to alarm the guards. "It's alright, Ora. Everything will be fine," assures Louise.

Just then, Samuel James, one of Long's men who defended the Smith family during the shooting enters the office waiting area. Ora looks up in surprise. Samuel walks over to Ora and says, "Ora Lewis, it's good to see you here. How are you?"

"I'm glad to see you as well. This is my father Nathan Lewis and the editor of my paper, Alonzo Willis," replies Ora.

Samuel shakes Alonzo's and Nathan's hands. "Ora, my name is Samuel James," he says.

"Samuel is the man who protected the Smith's from Walmsley's men during the shooting at City Hall," explains Ora.

"Well, Samuel it's very nice to meet you," says Alonzo. Samuel reaches over to shake Louise's hand.

"Well, I have to get going, but I just wanted to say hello. I hope your meeting with Senator Long is a good one," Samuel says as he walks out to the hall to continue securing the area.

"So, you're Ora Lewis from the City Hall shooting," says Margaret. "I've heard a lot about you." Ora blushes. "Senator Long will be out in a moment," Margaret says. Margaret's phone rings and she answers it, "Hello?"

"Send Alonzo and the group in to my office," says Long. He hangs up the phone.

Margaret stands up and walks toward Alonzo. "Long will see you now," she says. "Follow me." Margaret leads them into the governor's office.

"Come on in and have a seat," says Long. Ora is amazed by the stature and size of Governor Allen's office. The many books that line the walls, his enormous desk and the stately furniture are more than impressive. When Long reaches over to shake Alonzo's hand, Ora is elated. Alonzo introduces Long to Nathan, then he looks over to Ora and she freezes in place.

"Ora, Ora?" asks Louise.

"I'm listening. I just can't believe I'm actually here," whispers Ora.

"Senator Long, I'd like to introduce you to Nathan's daughter, Ora Lewis," says Alonzo.

Long extends his hand to greet Ora and says, "It's

very nice to meet you, Ora."

"Senator Long, it's an honor to meet you," Ora says as she shakes Long's hand. Alonzo takes a seat next to Louise and Nathan sits down next to Ora.

"Ora, I've heard a good deal about you already. Samuel James is so impressed with the work that you did for the Smith family. He said he's never seen a young girl do so much so quickly in an emergency," Long says.

"Senator Long, I have copies of our paper with coverage of Ora and the shooting right here for you," says Alonzo as he hands the paper to Long.

"This is exactly what I've been waiting for. So many of the papers have only reported the nonsense that Walmsley concocted," says Long as he flips through the pages of the Sepia Socialite newspaper. "These photographs are wonderful. I'm so glad that you're here."

"I would have mailed the paper to you sooner, but I wanted you to receive it in person," says Alonzo.

"Alonzo, your coverage of Walmsley and the shooting is priceless. You've deserved an award for years now," Long says.

"I do my best. When the news is good and we have someone like Ora to write about, the Sepia Socialite really outshines the rest," says Alonzo.

"We need a lot more issues of your paper like this one to counter Walmsley," Long says.

"If it were up to Ora, we'd always critique Walmsley," says Alonzo.

Long notices the articles written by Ora on the Smith's and on Walmsley. "Ora, your strong stance against Walmsley is to be commended. Alonzo is so fortunate to have you," says Long.

"I've never been afraid of Walmsley and now we've caught his racist followers in a very public attack. We're all fortunate to be alive," says Ora.

"You're right about that. Walmsley is more dangerous than even you realize. Follow Alonzo's lead and be very careful," advises Long.

"Senator Long, I hope I'm not too late to cover your candidacy for president," says Alonzo.

"Well, we're really just getting started," says Huey.

"So, what is your plan to reach people across the country?" asks Alonzo.

"The Share Our Wealth clubs have over seven million members nationwide. These members will organize canvassing across the country for our campaign," replies

Long.

"That's an excellent strategy," says Alonzo.

"When I speak to the press, I usually reach twenty-five million listeners on the radio alone. That's why I'm so active with reporters," says Long.

"Well, you've certainly won me over, Senator Long. Could we take a photo of you for the paper?" asks Alonzo.

"Of course," replies Huey as he walks over to his window for the photograph. Louise follows Long, carrying her camera. Long smiles for the picture. He has a political smile for these moments. It's a bit more polished than his natural expression. He doesn't blink for the flash, because he's so used to having his picture taken.

"Thank you, Senator Long," says Louise.

"It's no problem at all. I'm glad to do it. Just make sure to mail copies of the paper to me with the article. I have a collection of good ones that keep me going," Long says. He returns to the chair behind the desk. Louise takes her seat next to Alonzo.

"So what would you say is the primary focus of your campaign for President?" asks Alonzo.

"I plan to finally bring an end to the economic recession by redistributing the wealth, providing good paying jobs and making education accessible to everyone," says Long.

"That's an excellent platform, Senator Long. Roosevelt clearly lifted his Second New Deal Social Security plan directly from your old-age pension plan," says Alonzo.

"Roosevelt is so afraid I'll beat him that he had the IRS and FBI investigate me," reveals Long.

"That's an abuse of his power. He's very intimidated by you," Alonzo says.

"Alonzo, you know what my campaign is really about. I'm fighting racist elitists like Walmsley. Roosevelt just doesn't understand how to deal with southerners and white supremacists the way that I have my entire life. He's just an outsider looking in," Long says.

"I've known that from the beginning. Nothing will ever change down South until the right man is in the White House," says Alonzo.

"Exactly, Alonzo. I don't need to run for president. I'm already doing so well. I just want to make a difference for the people," says Long.

"Well, that's what I'll print, Senator Long," states Alonzo.

"Alonzo, the man who tried to force himself into our office this morning is one of many opponents who have tried everything to stop me," says Long.

"Do your guards recognize him? What faction is he from?" asks Alonzo.

"He's a member of the Square Deal Association, the group that attacked the East Baton Rouge courthouse in January," replies Long.

"That was a horrible attack. Baton Rouge was stunned," says Nathan.

"Yes we were, Nathan. This man is one of the few who wasn't arrested from the group. He's demanding my impeachment, but he's just making a spectacle of himself," says Long.

"He didn't get very far. I'm surprised that he made it into the capitol building at all," says Alonzo.

"He probably entered under the cover of one of my opponents in the legislature," says Long.

"There are so many factions that oppose your policies. You have to be vigilant," says Alonzo.

"Alonzo, the faction that most concerns me is the White League and Walmsley. They're a group of ruthless killers," says Long.

"I know they're very dangerous, but we've been able to handle them so far," says Alonzo.

"Alonzo and Nathan, can I confide in you?" asks Long.

"Yes of course," says Nathan.

"Absolutely," says Alonzo.

"I need to know that I can trust all of you," insists Long. Louise and Ora nod their heads in agreement. Long leans back in the chair and takes a moment to gather his thoughts. "Alonzo, Mayor Thomas Semmes Walmsley was caught with former Louisiana governors John Parker and Jared Sanders plotting my assassination in July," reveals Long. They're shocked. They knew that Walmsley was an enemy of Long, but they didn't understand the severity of the hatred.

"Now I know how treacherous Walmsley really is. He's one of the most dangerous political leaders in the state of Louisiana," says Alonzo.

"He'll stop at nothing to get rid of me," says Long.

"I am sorry, Senator Long. We had no idea," says Louise.

"Louise, it's alright. My guards just consider Walmsley another rogue assassin. There are many of them throughout the state who meet and plan my death," says Long.

"But Walmsley has now been caught plotting a murder. He shouldn't be allowed to serve as mayor any longer," says Alonzo.

"You're right, but we only have one witness. We don't have any solid evidence of his involvement," Long says.

"Senator Long, I will do everything in my power to stop Walmsley, even if it means having to take big risks," says Alonzo.

"Alonzo, I will do everything in my power to fight Walmsley and Jim Crow segregation," replies Long.

"That means a lot to us, Senator Long. Without you, the state would be chaotic. Your leadership is vital," says Alonzo.

"Segregation is like a slipknot that tightens its grip on Blacks and white liberals to death. It seems harmless on its face, but it is often fatal. I do the little things to challenge the establishment, but I need men like you and Nathan to prove supremacists wrong," says Long.

"Your words are very powerful. We're taking you for granted here in Louisiana. There's never been a presidential candidate quite like you, Senator Long," says Alonzo.

"I've seen lynchings and burnings throughout my forty-one years, Alonzo. I never realized that I'd have the power to fight white supremacists at this level. I always knew that I would somehow do something about it," says Long.

"This is why you have our support one hundred percent, Senator Long. We will begin our endorsement of your campaign immediately," says Alonzo.

"Every little bit helps, Alonzo," Long says.

"We will do our part to win the support of the Black community in New Orleans despite the hardships to our voting rights access," says Alonzo.

"Alonzo, you're going to face direct attacks from Walmsley when you publicize your support for my campaign. You now know how vicious he is, so don't be surprised if it gets physical. Stay in contact with my office regularly from now on," Long says.

"We're prepared for the worst, Senator Long. Walmsley is just one of so many racist leaders in the region who hound me," Alonzo says.

"If you put constant pressure on Walmsley about his

segregationist deeds, you'll break through his veil of lies and secrecy in a way that he cannot defend," says Long.

"I'm just not sure that he'll allow himself to be so easily exposed. He'll dodge every accusation and pretend to be fair and intelligent as he always does," urges Alonzo.

"Take a stand and don't look back, Alonzo. People will take notice and support you in a way that they never have before. Just trust me this time," says Long.

"You're right about Walmsley. No matter how vindictive he may be, he'll bend over backwards to make a good impression. If I fight hard enough, he may eventually give in," says Alonzo.

"You know Walmsley has lost a lot of support recently. He's much more vulnerable than you realize," Long says.

"Well, I won't hold back anymore. It's now or never with Walmsley. He'll be very angry, but he's already made his position clear on segregation," says Alonzo.

"That's it, Alonzo. Now is the time," says Long. "I would like to invite you all to return during a special session of the legislature on Sunday, September 8th. It will be a big day for me and I'd be so glad to have you here."

"Thank you, Senator Long. Your invitation means a

great deal to me," says Ora.

"I gladly accept your invitation to return in September," Nathan says.

"We'll definitely be here for you, Senator Long," says Alonzo.

"Well then, it's confirmed. You can meet with me here in my office just before I enter the House of Representatives. We can celebrate the passage of several bills when I return. It will be a long day for you, but you'll be able to cover the legislative activity," says Long.

"That would be wonderful. Thank you for inviting us to return," says Alonzo.

"It's the least I could do considering all you've done for me, Alonzo," Long says.

Governor Allen enters the office. "Good morning everyone," he says.

"Come on in. I'd like to introduce you to Alonzo Willis, Nathan Lewis, Louise Willis and Ora Lewis," says Long.

"Ora Lewis, I've heard good things about you. You're an exceptional young lady," says Allen as he shakes Ora's hand. "Alonzo, I feel like we've already met," Allen says as he shakes Alonzo's hand. Allen shakes Nathan's and

Louise's hands and greets them. "Huey, I need to speak with you about the Square Deal Association intruder privately," says Allen. He walks over to the desk.

"Well, Alonzo, our meeting has been cut short for the day. When you return in September we can get caught up on Walmsley," Long says.

"I hope to have a lot more good news for you then," Alonzo says as he stands up. Ora, Louise and Nathan follow Alonzo out to the waiting area.

"We were glad to have you today," says Margaret.

"The meeting was one of our best so far," says Alonzo. "Have a good day, Margaret."

"We'll be back on September 8th," Louise says.

"I'll mark it down on my calendar," says Margaret.

"Ora and Nathan will be here as well," Louise says.

"I'll make a note of that now," Margaret says. Alonzo opens the door for Ora and Louise. They follow him down the hall to the exit doors. "That was a powerful meeting," says Alonzo.

"Can you believe that he was so candid with us?" asks Louise.

"I never imagined he would share that kind of information with us today," says Ora.

"Long has always been very honest with me, but even I'm surprised by what he shared," Alonzo says.

"Alonzo and Louise, lunch is waiting for us at my house. Are you ready to eat?" asks Nathan.

"I did really work up an appetite this morning. Let's head over there now," says Alonzo. "We'll follow you to the house." They walk over to their cars. Nathan drives in front of Alonzo on their way out of the capitol building parking lot. They head to Scotlandville, where Nathan lives and works near Southern University.

"Nathan was pretty quiet this morning. I guess he has a lot to think about," Alonzo says.

"Don't we all?" asks Louise.

Nathan pulls into his driveway and Alonzo parks in front of the house. Nathan walks over to Alonzo's car and says, "Come on in. My wife and daughters have been waiting for you." Nathan leads them into the house.

Ida Lewis, Nathan's wife greets him and gives Ora a hug. Ora's younger sisters Shirley, Juanita and Luverne also greet her. Ida greets Alonzo and Louise, welcoming them to their home. Ida asks Nathan, "How was your meeting with Senator Long? Is he as charismatic as he seems in the news?"

"He's much more sharp and intelligent than he appears to be. He was very personable," replies Nathan.

"Well, come on in and have a seat here at the dining room table," says Ida. "I hope you like grilled redfish and long grain and wild rice, Alonzo and Louise."

"That sounds and looks delicious," says Alonzo.

"We're lucky that I didn't cook today. My meals are always so bland," says Louise as everyone laughs.

"So tell me everything there is to know about the meeting with Long," insists Ida.

Nathan takes her hand and pulls her off to the side. "Ida, I'll fill you in on the details later tonight once the girls are in bed. Long said some things that were very disturbing," he says.

Ida frowns and holds Nathan. "I had no idea. I'm so sorry for asking," she says.

"You're fine. I just have a lot to think about with Ora now," Nathan says. "So who's hungry?" asks Nathan smiling at Alonzo and Louise. Ida rushes to serve the guests.

"One good thing about our meeting with Long today is that I began my coverage of his campaign for the presidency," says Alonzo.

"That's very good news," says Ida.

"He's not intimidated at all by President Roosevelt, despite his personal attacks," says Alonzo.

"Yes, Long even revealed that Roosevelt had him investigated by the FBI and the IRS. They found nothing on Long but pure heart," says Nathan.

"I can't believe that President Roosevelt would misuse his power that way. It's very disappointing," says Ida.

"President Roosevelt is a good man. Long poses a threat that he just can't handle," says Nathan.

"Roosevelt has worked hard and he does care about Black people. He just doesn't care the way that Long cares about the South," says Alonzo.

"I supported Roosevelt from the beginning, but after today, my support is for Senator Long," says Nathan.

"Ora, we're all very proud of you and your writing. Everything has happened so quickly for you," says Ida.

"Thank you, Ida. It's been a real blessing," Ora says. They finish their meals. Ida and Ora clear the table.

Nathan and Alonzo walk outside to the front porch to talk. "Alonzo, considering everything that was said by Long in today's meeting, I'm concerned about Ora and the dangers of covering Walmsley," says Nathan.

"I know you must be very concerned about Walmsley. I assure you that I will limit her coverage of him and I will keep a close eye on her," says Alonzo.

"Thank you again for giving Ora an opportunity to write for the Sepia Socialite," says Nathan.

"Nathan, I know you have a lot on your mind that I thought you would actually share with Senator Long today," says Alonzo.

"You know I hoped to discuss segregation in Baton Rouge with Long, but the meeting ended abruptly," says Nathan.

"The intruder is just another Baton Rouge white supremacist. They're everywhere. The conditions in Baton Rouge are just as bad as New Orleans despite Long's presence here," Nathan says.

"There's so much work to be done in Baton Rouge, but I'm inundated with cases in New Orleans," says Alonzo.

"Although I didn't have an opportunity to discuss Baton Rouge segregation with Senator Long, I'd like to write articles on it for the Sepia Socialite," says Nathan.

"That would be great, Nathan. You're welcome to

write as much as you can about segregation here," says Alonzo. Ora walks outside to the porch and greets Alonzo and Nathan. Ida offers Alonzo some pecan pie and he sits down inside at the table next to Louise.

Nathan says to Ora, "You now know how dangerous Walmsley is, Ora. Do not write another article on the mayor."

"Papa, Walmsley won't attack me. Alonzo has never been attacked for what he's written," says Ora.

"Ora, I'd like you to remain in Baton Rouge with us until Long can get Walmsley under control. I am very concerned about you," Nathan warns.

"Papa, I promise to focus on segregation and avoid Walmsley from now on," insists Ora.

"Ora, you know I support your efforts to fight for desegregation as a writer, but you must avoid confrontation with Walmsley," says Nathan.

"Papa, I've worked so hard for acceptance from Alonzo, because of you. We can't give up on Alonzo now," says Ora.

"You're right, Ora. There's a reason that we're all here today, and I have to accept the risks that come with your success," says Nathan.

"Would the two of you also like some pecan pie?" asks Ida interrupting Nathan.

"That would be a nice treat to calm my mind," replies Nathan. Ora and Nathan walk inside and have a seat next to Alonzo and Louise. "Alonzo, can you imagine the expression on President Roosevelt's face when he sees the front page stories about Senator Long's run for president?" he asks. Everyone laughs.

"He's got a big surprise waiting for him in the White House," Alonzo says. Ida is relieved to hear Nathan and Alonzo laugh together. She tries to think of a way to lighten the mood. Ida walks over to their radio in the living room. She turns the radio on and hears Louis Armstrong's "Basin Street Blues."

Nathan hears the song and says, "Turn it up so we can hear it, Ida." Nathan walks over to Ida and grabs her waist. He begins to dance with her. Alonzo and Louise join them in the living room and dance as well. Ora dances with her sisters. Nathan turns off the radio as the song concludes and says, "Ida, Senator Long has invited us to meet with him again on September 8th here in Baton Rouge."

"Oh my. That's wonderful news. You really made a great impression on Senator Long today," says Ida.

"Long was open with us today. We'd probably still be there if governor Allen hadn't interrupted our meeting," says Nathan.

"Did he give you a reason for the interruption?" asks Ida.

"A white supremacist tried to break into the governor's office, just before Long welcomed us in. Governor Allen needed to meet with Senator Long about the incident," replies Nathan.

"You were fortunate to meet with Long at all today," says Ida.

"Yes we were," says Alonzo.

"Were you able to actually meet governor Allen?" asks Ida.

"Governor Allen introduced himself to us all, but we didn't have an opportunity to meet with him," replies Nathan.

"Ida, thank you for this wonderful meal. Redfish is one of my favorites. Nathan, thank you for joining us today at the meeting," says Alonzo.

"Alonzo, today has been much better than expected. You're welcome to return in September or any time you're in Baton Rouge," says Nathan. Alonzo, Louise and Ora walk out to the front porch. Nathan, Ida and the girls follow them outside.

"Well, Nathan and Ida, we're headed back down to New Orleans," says Alonzo. Ora kisses her sisters goodbye. Ida embraces Ora and says, "Try to call us more often."

"I will. I know Papa is worried," says Ora.

"Ora, if the situation in New Orleans becomes too dangerous, I'm only a phone call away," says Nathan.

"Papa, I understand. Try to worry less and pray more," says Ora. She gives her father a hug. Alonzo and Louise climb into his car. Ora waves goodbye to Nathan and her sisters, then enters Alonzo's car.

"Your father and Ida lifted my spirits. They're very special people," says Alonzo.

"My father and Ida are concerned about us now that he's met with Long. He'd like me to live in Baton Rouge with him until Long stops Walmsley," Ora says.

"Well, I'm so glad that you're returning to New Orleans with us," says Alonzo.

"I let him know how important it is for me to write for you in New Orleans. He said he'll take it day by day," Ora says. Alonzo drives through Scotlandville toward the River Road.

"Ora, there may be some turmoil and even attacks, but we'll never compromise your safety," says Louise.

"I'm very upset about Walmsley's assassination attempt. I had no idea that he despised Long so deeply," Ora says.

"We know about the fighting, but the assassination is much more than we expected today. Long has been so patient with Walmsley. He could have him impeached as mayor," says Louise.

"Long is being careful about his approach to Walmsley. He hasn't publicized the assassination attempt and he hasn't responded to Walmsley's defense of Dean Eiffel," Alonzo says.

"Long's method of dealing with his opponents is brilliant. He has a way of facing adversity that's cunning," Ora says.

"When Long ran for Senate, he outmaneuvered Senator Joseph Ransdall during his campaign. Ransdall never had a chance against Long," says Alonzo.

"Long is a strategist and he was born to win," Ora says.

"Long has a genuine interest in working with us to stop Walmsley. There's a great deal more at stake for him than we really know," says Louise.

Alonzo turns onto the River Road toward New Orleans. "I would like us to shift our focus from Walmsley to Long in the next few issues of the Sepia Socialite," says Alonzo.

"That's a good plan," Louise says.

"I would love to write about the work that Long is doing for the country," Ora says.

"Walmsley will still be very upset about our coverage, but we won't give him any reasons to fight with us about Dean Eiffel or anything he's done," Alonzo says.

"Walmsley will be completely thrown off by our endorsement of Long for president and the change in our upbeat tone," Louise says.

"Walmsley may try to regain the attention of the press, but we won't respond to his rhetoric," Alonzo says.

"We can begin with today's interview and photograph and fill the paper with stories on Long's work to provide education to Black and white students alike," Louise says.

"We will completely counter Walmsley's lies and attacks," says Alonzo.

"Walmsley won't stop his Jim Crow antics, but he

won't have fuel for the fire from us any longer," Ora says.

"It's just for a short time, Ora. We'll pick up where we left off in a few weeks," Alonzo says.

"That will give us all time to regroup and plan our next moves," Louise says. Alonzo nears St. Gabriel.

Ora doesn't notice the plantations along the way, because she's focused on Senator Long. She's still very excited about the day. "Will we cover Long now through September when we meet with him again?" asks Ora.

"That's what I have in mind," replies Alonzo. "I'd like you to write an article about what you experienced today with Long, Ora."

"That would be great. I'm very interested in supporting Senator Long's campaign for president," Ora says.

"This is a major commitment, Alonzo. We have our work cut out for us," Louise says.

"We most certainly do. Encouraging Black people to vote for Long despite the harassment and attacks from racist officials is the biggest challenge," says Alonzo.

"Our coverage will have to include voting rights articles," Louise says.

"They must and I know that Walmsley will be very

angry. We'll be prepared for him this time," says Alonzo.

"It seems that everything we write agitates Walmsley," Ora says.

"Our very existence is a threat to Walmsley's power. He despises Black journalists," Alonzo says. He drives through Saint James Parish within miles of New Orleans. The River Road is relatively quiet with light traffic on the thoroughfares. Alonzo is able to breeze through the small communities. "I have a plan to throw Walmsley completely off. After we meet with Long again we'll compare Walmsley's administration to the Long administration. We'll dissect Walmsley policy by policy."

"Could we begin that coverage immediately?" asks Ora.

Alonzo laughs and replies, "I would, but we need time to let Walmsley cool down. He's angry and on edge right now. I wouldn't want to compromise our integrity," replies Alonzo.

"It seems that nothing can stop Walmsley," Ora says.

"New Orleans is under siege with Walmsley in office. That doesn't mean he's completely unstoppable. Long has taken away much of his financial power.

Walmsley's powerful opponents are just waiting for him to finally give in," says Alonzo.

"Walmsley will eventually release his grip on the city. We must expose him. It will take a miracle, but it's not impossible," Louise says.

"Walmsley is like so many Jim Crow mayors across the country. Even Roosevelt has not been able to change their mindset. Black people have no recourse," Alonzo says.

"When Walmsley does eventually leave, a new era will begin for Blacks in the South, beginning with New Orleans," says Louise.

"Just imagine if Walmsley was gone and Long was president. The South would never be the same," says Alonzo.

"Just getting rid of Walmsley would be tremendous. I almost can't imagine how wonderful it would be for Senator Long to be president," Ora says.

"Imagine having everything you could ever need and want and more. That's what Long's Share Our Wealth plan would mean for Americans, Black and white," says Alonzo.

"Long would take the steps that Roosevelt hasn't to

finally bring an end to Jim Crow segregation in America," says Louise.

Alonzo approaches Jefferson Parish and Metairie. The traffic is heavy and the city is bustling. Alonzo is able to slowly make his way back to New Orleans. "That's why we have to work twice as hard to ensure Long's victory. There's so much at stake for us and we have to let the people know it," he says.

"Senator Long is a great person, and he'd make a great president," Ora says.

"Ora, it's going to take a lot of work. People are not ready to change their way of life to keep pace with Long," Alonzo says.

"Most people are pleased with President Roosevelt. They don't yet understand the difference," Louise says.

"Roosevelt is a great man. He just views the world differently," says Ora.

"Roosevelt's view of the world is a good one. He just doesn't challenge southern racism the way that Long does," says Alonzo. He makes it to New Orleans and turns onto Claiborne Avenue uptown.

"I really wish that Roosevelt could work together with Long to bring an end to segregation," Ora says.

"That would definitely be good, Ora, but Roosevelt is just not willing to treat Long with the respect that he deserves. It's all or nothing for Long," Louise says.

"Long and Roosevelt oppose each other so strongly, because Long plans to redistribute the wealth of the super rich. Roosevelt comes from a wealthy family and many of his supporters are very wealthy. Long represents a belief that threatens Roosevelt's way of life," explains Alonzo. He drives through downtown New Orleans and he reaches Tulane Avenue. A New Orleans policeman begins to follow Alonzo in his patrol car. The policeman pulls Alonzo over.

"What's happening? Did you do something wrong?" asks Louise in distress.

"Just remain calm and don't make any sudden moves, Louise and Ora," replies Alonzo.

The policeman approaches Alonzo's window and says, "Alonzo Willis, please exit the car. I need to see your identification." Louise and Ora look at each other in dismay.

Alonzo opens his car door and stands in front of the policeman. He reads the policeman's badge. "Officer Poche, have I done something wrong?" Alonzo asks.

"You met with Huey P. Long today, haven't you?" asks Thomas Poche.

"I didn't know that meeting with the U.S. Senator was a crime," replies Alonzo.

"What was the nature of the meeting?" Thomas asks.

"I am a journalist and I'm covering Senator Long's campaign for the presidency," Alonzo replies.

"I've been informed of something different. I understand that you met with Senator Long about segregation," says Thomas.

Alonzo is surprised. He stares at the policeman for a moment and realizes that Walmsley has orchestrated this scene. Alonzo says, "If I've broken the law, then name the crime that I've committed."

Thomas opens his ticketing book and begins to write a citation on Alonzo. "You have been loitering, Alonzo. Here is your citation," says Thomas as he hands the ticket to him.

"This is very unfortunate, Officer Poche. I have done nothing wrong," says Alonzo.

"Alonzo, it's time to get going. I don't want to have to cite you for questioning my authority," says Thomas.

Alonzo opens his car door and climbs back in. Thomas walks back to his car and drives away. "Can you believe this policeman and the nerve of Mayor Walmsley? He just won't stop," Alonzo says. "I'm so sorry you had to see that, Ora. Walmsley set it up to scare us all. Are you alright?" he asks.

"I can't believe Mayor Walmsley would have you pulled over for meeting with Senator Long about segregation. He'll stop at nothing," replies Ora.

"Let's get you back home right away. I have to call Senator Long and let him know what happened. Try not to worry, Ora," Alonzo says.

"I'm not worried. I'm just disappointed. How can we defend ourselves against Walmsley?" asks Ora.

"Ora, we now know that Walmsley is aware of our meeting with Long. He's watching everything that we're doing. Alonzo handled it well," says Louise.

Alonzo starts his car and drives toward Annette Street. He's a little upset, but he's relieved that the stop didn't escalate. "That stop was a warning. I'm not so worried about it. If we focus our coverage and attention on Long, Walmsley will be disarmed," Alonzo says.

"It's more than just a warning. It's a threat to

desegregation," says Louise.

"It's all about segregation, Louise. It's Walmsley's power structure and twisted platform. Without it, he's lost," says Alonzo.

"If you had asked the police officer who sent him, he might have actually admitted that it was Walmsley. There are no boundaries," says Ora.

"Walmsley's days as mayor are numbered. Long will soon stop him," Louise says.

"Well for now, we'll avoid Walmsley and his hostility," says Alonzo. He turns left onto Annette Street and parks at Ora's curb.

"Ora, today was still a good one for us. I hope you're not too discouraged," says Louise.

"I'm fine. I just have to gather my thoughts tonight. I'll be ready for work tomorrow morning," Ora replies.

"We'll be here for you bright and early in the morning," says Alonzo.

"Working will keep my mind off of the police stop and Walmsley's attacks," Ora says.

"Ora, the harder we work, the closer we'll come to getting rid of Walmsley. You shouldn't regret the work that you've done just because he's trying to intimidate us," says

Louise.

"Well, thank you, Alonzo and Louise. I'll see you tomorrow," Ora says as she steps out of the car and walks to her front door. Alonzo and Louise wave goodbye and Alonzo drives back down to Claiborne Avenue. Ora opens her front door and enters.

"Ora, you made it home. How was the meeting with the great Huey P. Long?" asks Josephine.

Ora walks over to embrace Josephine and Ellis. "I'm just so glad to be home," she says.

"A hug? What's going on here?" asks Ellis.

"Ma Mere and Ma Mum, Mayor Walmsley is much more dangerous than I realized," replies Ora.

"You're back, Ora. How was it?" Cleo asks walking into the kitchen.

"Yeah, how was Senator Huey P. Long?" asks Alexia as she sits down at the kitchen table.

"Hi, Cleo and Alexia. Huey P. Long was great. It's the things he shared about his opponents that clouded the day," explains Ora.

"Were you able to introduce yourself to Long?" asks Josephine.

"Yes, of course. Long knew all about the Smith's

and the City Hall shooting," replies Ora.

"So he mentioned Walmsley?" asks Josephine.

"Long said so much more about Walmsley than we thought he would," replies Ora.

"So, what really happened, Ora?" asks Cleo.

"One of Long's opponents tried to force his way into Long's office, screaming and yelling that Long should be impeached," describes Ora.

"There's so much of that going on these days, especially with Long everywhere in the news," says Josephine.

"Long's guards must have taught him a lesson," Cleo says.

"The man was arrested and put out of the capitol building," says Ora.

"Did you have any trouble getting into the building at all?" asks Ellis.

"No, Alonzo made sure that everything was taken care of," replies Ora.

"I would have liked to have been there with you and Papa. Long is one of my favorite leaders," says Alexia.

"Cleo and Alexia, Long's guard who protected the Smith family at City Hall was there today. His name is

Samuel James. He introduced himself to everyone and said some very nice things about me," says Ora.

"He's my kind of guy," says Cleo.

"Once the guards cleared the area, Long was ready to meet with us," says Ora.

"Did he invite you into his office or just speak with you outside?" asks Josephine.

"Long really allowed us to meet in Governor Allen's office privately," replies Ora.

"So what was so bad about what he said?" asks Josephine.

"Ma Mere, Cleo, Alexia, please try to keep this between us," Ora says as she pauses and folds her hands on the kitchen table.

"Take your time, honey. It's alright. You don't have to tell us if you don't want to," consoles Ellis.

"Ma Mere, Long's guard caught Walmsley in a meeting with two former governors plotting his assassination in July," reveals Ora.

"Oh, my word. That's unbelievable," says Josephine.

"And Walmsley's still a free man?" asks Ellis.

"Now I understand why Long's men were carrying

guns at City Hall. The mayor is a killer," Cleo says.

"I'm shocked. I knew Walmsley was a bad mayor, but I didn't realize that he was a murderer. What are we going to do?" asks Alexia.

"Walmsley even had Alonzo stopped by a policeman on his way here to the house. The policeman questioned him about our meeting with Long," reveals Ora.

"Ora, I'm so sorry you had to experience that," says Josephine.

"You have to be very careful. Try to take it slow from now on," Ellis says.

"Was Alonzo arrested?" Cleo asks.

"No, the policeman gave him a citation for loitering, and let us go with a warning," replies Ora.

"This has been a tough day for you. You're right in the middle of a big fight," Alexia says.

"I don't know what I would have done if the police had stopped me," says Cleo.

"Walmsley is so angry right now that he could really hurt us. Alonzo is going to stop covering him for the rest of the month," Ora says.

"Well, try to unwind and get ready for dinner. You can give your father a call before we eat," says Ellis. Ora walks down the hall into the bathroom. She closes the door behind her and stares into the mirror. Ora smiles, then presses her cheeks. She turns on the water to wash her face, then slashes some water into her mouth.

"What's going on in there, girl? Are you trying to hide from us?" says Cleo knocking on the bathroom door.

"I'm not hiding. I'm just trying to freshen up," responds Ora.

"Well, hurry up. We're all waiting for you," says Cleo.

Ora gets undressed and takes a quick shower. She wraps herself in a towel and heads down the hall to her room. Ora puts on her pajamas and robe. She walks out to the living room and picks up the phone to call her dad. The phone rings and Nathan answers, "Hello?"

"Papa, it's Ora," she says.

"That was fast. What's on your mind?" asks Nathan.

"Papa, Alonzo was stopped by a policeman on the way to our house," explains Ora.

"Why would a policeman stop Alonzo?" asks Nathan.

"Walmsley sent the policeman to interrogate Alonzo. He knew all about the meeting with Long. He asked Alonzo about segregation," replies Ora.

"That's alright, Ora. It's just part of the job. You know how I feel about you being there, but I have to trust Alonzo this time," Nathan says.

"I'm glad, Papa," Ora says. "It wasn't so bad."

"Yeah, well let's keep you out of trouble," says Nathan.

"Papa, I'm running out of courage. I just don't know how to stop Walmsley," she says.

"Ora, do you remember how hard it was to get Alonzo to publish your letter criticizing Walmsley? Alonzo knew how dangerous he was and you wouldn't give up," Nathan says.

"Yes, Papa, I remember," says Ora.

"Well, that's the innocence and bravery you need to have to bring an end to Walmsley. It will never be easy, but you won't regret your decision to take a stand," says Nathan.

"Papa, I can't believe you're still encouraging me after today," says Ora.

"You're my baby girl. I'll never let anything happen to you as long as I'm alive," says Nathan.

"I love you, Papa," Ora says.

"I love you too. Now try to get some rest and call me back tomorrow with good news," Nathan says.

"Good night, Papa," says Ora.

"Good night, Ora," Nathan says as he gently hangs up the phone. Ora hangs up the phone and walks over to the kitchen table.

"So what did he say?" asks Josephine.

"He said that I should be brave and trust Alonzo," replies Ora.

"That sounds like the Nathan I know," says Josephine.

"Dinner smells so good," Cleo says as Ellis pulls a roast beef tenderloin from the oven.

"I'm glad I made it home for dinner," says Ora.

"We cooked this especially for your big day," Ellis says.

"I was famished. This is the meal I needed," Alexia says. Josephine and Ellis serve the food. Ora, Cleo and Alexia are elated. They laugh and joke about their day at work. Ora enjoys the time with her family, then falls asleep with a clear mind and no regrets.

CHAPTER 5 / "A POLITICAL FIRE"

"Ida, your crab gumbo is delicious. The shrimp stuffed mirliton is succulent. I'm so glad to be here this weekend with you all," says Ora.

"It's always nice to have you here, Ora. We all really miss you," says Ida.

"Everything turned out so well with Alonzo last month. I'm glad that I decided to let you stay in New Orleans," Nathan says.

"Once Alonzo shifted the focus of his coverage to Huey P. Long's campaign for president, the Sepia Socialite became the talk of the town," says Ora.

"Alonzo really made me proud when he published my articles on Baton Rouge segregation," Nathan says.

"A lot of readers have called in about your articles. They've been so surprised to learn about what's happening up here," Ora says.

"Isn't that interesting? I always assumed that everyone knew about the white supremacist attacks in Baton Rouge. I'll try to write as much as I can for Alonzo from now on," says Nathan.

"That's really good news, Ora. Sometimes we feel like we're in isolation here with no outlet," Ida says.

"Well, you're not alone anymore. A lot of people in New Orleans and the surrounding area are listening very closely to Papa now," Ora says.

"There's so much freedom in being able to write about segregation here without the racist leaders knowing about my articles, at least not immediately," Nathan says.

"Your articles are in the right hands with Huey P. Long and Oscar K. Allen," says Ora.

"Ora did you enjoy Reverend Wire's sermon this morning?" asks Nathan.

"Reverend Wire's prayers for Huey P. Long about

life and death were very moving, Papa," replies Ora.

"Reverend Wire's message was very meaningful for us considering all that we know about the attacks against Long," Nathan says.

"Reverend Wire's message rings true for segregation and death threats in Baton Rouge as well," says Ora.

"He's is a profound minister who sees beyond the confines of social status and race," says Nathan.

"Ora, you're doing so well now despite the attacks from Mayor Walmsley. Your coverage of Long has been very thorough," says Ida.

"Looking beyond Walmsley has been liberating. I was too focused on Walmsley to realize how much good Long has done for the state," says Ora.

"That's right, Ora. You hadn't yet begun to enjoy the good works of Huey P. Long, because you burdened yourself with Walmsley's antics," says Nathan.

"Alonzo and Louise are so relieved to escape the lopsided boxing match with Walmsley. I've never seen them so excited about writing as they are now," says Ora.

"I didn't realize how close Alonzo was to Long. He has a powerful connection," Nathan says.

"Alonzo and Louise are unassuming. They probably know several top politicians in Louisiana and other states as well," Ora says.

"Alonzo has always been well connected. That's why his paper is so well respected in the region. He also works closely with the National Association for the Advancement of Colored People," says Nathan.

"Yes, I know, Papa. He's one of the leading members in New Orleans," says Ora.

"That's why I've encouraged you to work so hard to join Alonzo's staff," says Nathan.

"I'm not yet a staff member, but he definitely welcomes my writing," says Ora.

"I'm just glad to see you back in school," Nathan says.

"School is tough now that I'm writing so often, but it's definitely worth the effort," says Ora.

"Now that's what I'd like to hear. Ora, I decided to bring you to Baton Rouge Friday so that we could enjoy the weekend with you," Nathan says.

"I'm glad you did. I feel much better about meeting with Long now that I've spent the weekend here, Papa," she says.

"That's what we hoped for. Sometimes it's good to take a break from the pressures of leadership," Nathan says.

"Ora, Long has such a strong chance of winning the presidency with the support from the press for his candidacy," Ida says.

"Ida, it will take continuous press coverage to earn the support of the voters, but it's not impossible," says Nathan.

"Papa, the people of Louisiana are so excited about Long's run for president. If the rest of the country is as energized as we are, he'll definitely win," Ora says.

"I wish that I could see the people's reactions to Long and Nathan's articles in New Orleans. That's wonderful, Ora," says Ida.

"It would be great for you and Papa to visit the Sepia Socialite office on release day. It's amazing to see the issues fly off of the shelves and the readers call in to express their support," Ora says.

"Maybe I could plan to visit one release day. I could show my support for your writing," Nathan says.

"You should visit next Friday. Just take the day off from work," suggests Ida.

"I'll check my schedule and let Alonzo know that

I'm planning to visit," Nathan says.

"Papa, are we prepared for Long tonight?" asks Ora.

"He'll likely want to know the status of your coverage of his campaign and segregation," replies Nathan.

"Alonzo has shipped issues of the paper to Long each week. Long knows all about our coverage of his campaign and your coverage of segregation in Baton Rouge," says Ora.

"It's very special for you to meet with Long about segregation in Baton Rouge today, because you've worked so hard for desegregation, Nathan," Ida says.

"The most important thing is that Long hears or reads my words and makes a conscious decision to take action," Nathan says. Ida clears the table for the family. Nathan, Ida and Ora walk over to the living room and turn on the radio for the evening news. The reporter says, "U.S. Senator Huey P. Long is in Baton Rouge for a special legislative session this evening. Senator Long has proposed 42 new bills to the Louisiana House of Representatives that further centralize his control over the state by creating several new state agencies. The bills also strip away the remaining powers of Mayor T. Semmes Walmsley of New Orleans." The radio signal beeps seven times and the reporter says, "U.S. Senator Huey P. Long has now read on the Louisiana Senate floor a transcript of a recording of a meeting where New Orleans Mayor T. Semmes Walmsley, Governor John Parker and Governor Jared Sanders plotted his assassination."

Nathan and Ida turn to each other in surprise. Nathan walks over to turn the radio off. "Long finally took a stand. It was very brave of him to expose Walmsley before the Louisiana Senate," says Nathan.

"It's such a relief to hear that Walmsley's assassination plot is no longer a secret," says Ora.

"I know that Long has a strategy to expose Walmsley," says Ida.

"Now Walmsley is on the defense publicly and his integrity is in question for the people of Louisiana," Nathan says.

"Long has shifted the focus of the legislature and the press to Walmsley's violent attacks," Ora says.

"I'm very interested in seeing Walmsley's reactions to Long's allegations. Walmsley won't be able to control the press and deflect Long's allegations this time the way that he always does," Nathan says.

"Long has effectively stopped Walmsley in his

tracks. He'll never recover from this one," says Ida.

"Let's hope that this is the beginning of the end for Walmsley," Nathan says.

"I would have loved to have covered the Walmsley assassination plot, but the story is on the live wire now," says Ora.

"Ora, I'm glad that you didn't release the story on Walmsley, because it's very dangerous coverage," Nathan says.

"Long handled Walmsley better than anyone in the press ever could. He's a genius," says Ora.

"It's up to the people of New Orleans to decide if Walmsley deserves to be mayor now that he's been exposed," says Ida.

"The people know who Walmsley is. They just don't have the strength to stop him," says Nathan.

"Papa, Walmsley won't be able to withstand the pressure, but he'll try to diffuse the situation just as he always does," says Ora.

"You're right, Ora. Just try to avoid covering Walmsley for as long as you can," insists Nathan.

"You know I will, but it's hard to ignore the headlines. If he wasn't so hostile, I'd be all over this story," says Ora.

"That's what concerns me. You'd ignore the warning signs if you could and put yourself in harm's way," Nathan says.

"Walmsley is an easy target. He's so full of hatred that he's unmistakably racist. He'll never change," says Ora.

"Ora, even Walmsley can change under the right circumstances. Just stay focused and pick your battles. The time will come for you to confront him peacefully," says Nathan.

"I believe you, Papa. I can be patient, especially when we're working so closely with Long," Ora says.

"Long will let us know tonight what he has in mind for Walmsley. He's thought about him a great deal and he knows what to do. Trust Long's strategy and listen to him carefully. He's the reason that Alonzo is so successful," Nathan says.

"Papa, can you imagine if I owned a newspaper or magazine of my own one day? I'd fight so hard for desegregation," says Ora.

"I know you will. When you work hard and finish school you'll have everything you're dreaming of including a new kindhearted mayor," Nathan says.

"I can just see the new mayor now. He'll be intelligent and fair. He'll work closely with Long and he'll fight for desegregation," Ora says.

"Yes he will, Ora. Don't give up on your vision," Nathan says.

"It's almost time for your meeting with Long, Nathan and Ora. You don't want to be late," Ida says. Ida hands Nathan his hat and jacket.

"Thank you, dear," Nathan says. Ora walks to her sisters' bedroom to gather her purse, then returns to the front door. "I'm ready to head over to the capitol building. Hopefully, Alonzo and Louise will be there waiting," says Nathan.

"They're always right on time," Ora says.

"I know that your meeting will go well tonight. I'll be praying for you," Ida says.

"We'll definitely need your prayers, Ida," says Nathan. Nathan and Ora walk out to the driveway toward his car. Nathan unlocks the car door for Ora and she climbs into the car. Nathan enters the car, then turns the ignition on. He backs out of the driveway onto Scotland Avenue toward Scenic Highway. "This meeting should be a good one," he says.

"Long will definitely be ready to make the next moves for his campaign in New Orleans," Ora says.

"That's the focus I'm hoping for," Nathan says.

"Long's campaign has been so popular for the paper that Alonzo and Louise have found a new purpose," Ora says.

"While Huey P. Long is still alive, he will give us a purpose to embrace," Nathan says. He turns onto North 3rd Street and approaches the capitol building guard.

The guard asks, "What are your names? Give me your identification."

"My name is Nathan Lewis and my daughter's name is Ora Lewis," Nathan replies as he hands his ID to the guard.

"I see you both here in our log. Senator Long is expecting you," says the guard as he lifts the barrier gate for Nathan. Nathan parks his car. He and Ora wait for Alonzo and Louise to arrive.

"Alonzo should be here soon. They're probably caught in traffic," Ora says.

"There's not much traffic tonight, Ora. Alonzo should've been here by now, especially considering the importance of the meeting," Nathan says.

"They're not late yet. Just give them a moment," insists Ora. Alonzo and Louise arrive and park next to Nathan.

"They're finally here. I wonder what took them so long," Nathan says.

"The River Road is difficult to travel at night. That's why Long has replaced it," replies Ora.

"Why didn't they leave early and meet us at the house?" asks Nathan.

Alonzo walks over to his car and says, "Nathan and Ora, we're glad to see that you're here early. We were delayed on our route. There was an accident that stopped the traffic on the River Road," explains Alonzo.

"We knew there was some sort of delay. We're relieved to see you," says Nathan.

"Let's head inside before it gets too late," says Ora.

"Ora, you look well rested. Have you enjoyed your weekend away from us?" asks Louise.

Ora smiles and says, "It's always good to be there with you writing. I've done a lot of thinking this weekend and I have some fresh ideas for articles."

"It's so quiet at the office without you there with us. Tonight's meeting is the highlight of the weekend," says

Louise. They enter the capitol building and walk toward the corridor and Governor Allen's office. They see Senator Long up ahead surrounded by his bodyguards. He is stopped just outside the office by a thin framed man wearing glasses and a white linen suit who approaches him to make an appeal.

"Senator Long, please hear me out. Judge Benjamin Pavy is a noble servant who has done nothing wrong. You mustn't redistrict the parishes he serves," pleads Dr. Carl Weiss.

Senator Long stares at Weiss and listens, then says, "The decision has been made. There is nothing that can be done at this late hour." Long turns and walks to the governor's office. Weiss lingers in the corridor suspiciously. Long enters the office leaving Weiss behind. Alonzo, Nathan, Louise and Ora make their way to Senator Long. They enter the office waiting area.

"Welcome, Alonzo. The Senator will need a few moments before he accepts you into his office. It's been a tough day," says Margaret Wright.

"Thank you, Margaret," Nathan says.

"It was so nice to see Senator Long out in the corridor, because he's likely doing well in the House of

Representatives tonight," Ora says.

"Long is unstoppable in the Louisiana legislature," says Alonzo.

"Long does so much for the state that's taken for granted," says Nathan.

"Long will do a great deal for the state as president," says Louise.

Long calls Margaret Wright who answers the phone and says, "Yes, Senator Long."

"Please bring Alonzo and the group into my office," he says.

"I'll bring them to you now," Margaret says as she hangs up the phone. Margaret approaches Alonzo and says, "Please follow me into the governor's office." She opens the door to the office for Alonzo and invites the group in.

Long says, "Welcome back, everyone. Please come on in and have a seat."

"Thank you, Senator Long," says Nathan.

"Alonzo, oh boy your coverage of my campaign has been nonstop. It's hotter than hot for the boys down in New Orleans," says Long.

"If you think that's something, take a look at Friday's issue of the paper," Alonzo says as he hands the newspaper to Long. He browses through the paper and he's very pleased with what he sees.

"This is more than I ever expected, Alonzo. You should be Editor of the *Times Picayune*."

"That's what I tell him, but he doesn't believe me," says Louise. Alonzo smiles.

"Senator Long, the issues of our paper featuring your campaign for the presidency have been the most popular issues ever printed," Alonzo says.

"I like the sound of that, Alonzo," says Long.

"If the sales of the paper are any indication of your chances of winning, you're sure to claim victory in the state of Louisiana," says Alonzo.

"The people love you, Senator Long," says Ora.

"My struggle is not so much with FDR as it is against my assassination plotting opponents. It will be a miracle if I actually serve until the November election," Long says.

"Everything will be fine, Senator Long. Trust the system that you've worked so hard to build," Alonzo says.

"We're just so glad that you publicly exposed Walmsley's assassination plot," says Nathan.

"Nathan, you're a very focused man. I've seen your

articles on Baton Rouge segregation in Alonzo's paper and I'd like to hear more from you," says Long.

"Senator Long, you've done so much already for us, but local leaders have blocked the progress of your policies throughout the state," Nathan says.

"Nathan, I'd like you to contact my office directly to keep me informed of issues that arise with segregation in Baton Rouge," says Long.

"I definitely will, Senator Long. Thank you for making it possible," Nathan says.

"Senator Long, Mayor Walmsley is backed into a corner now that you've released information on his assassination plot to the press," Alonzo says.

"Let's hope so, Alonzo. There's no limit to how far Walmsley will take it when it comes to a political fight. This time I didn't bite my tongue and Walmsley was completely exposed," says Long.

"You timed the release perfectly just as Walmsley was being inundated with coverage of your campaign," Alonzo says.

"Alonzo, I would have invited you to release the story, but I knew it would be too dangerous for you," Long says.

"The White League would have attacked us. The story never would have reached the top news sources in time. You made the right decision, Senator Long," Alonzo replies.

"Walmsley is sure to resign soon. A new day is dawning in New Orleans for everyone including Blacks," Long says.

"Senator Long, you've truly inspired so many people. Your work will never be forgotten," says Ora.

"Ora, you are a special young woman. I can see why Alonzo lets you stick around," says Long.

"Thank you, Senator Long. That means a lot to me as her father," says Nathan.

"Tonight's special session is certainly another success for you. It's such a privilege to be here this evening," Alonzo says.

"The special session has gone very well. All 42 bills proposed will likely be passed. I am concerned about one particular bill though," Long says.

"What's that?" asks Alonzo.

"There is someone here tonight who approached me about one bill and I'm disappointed that he's here," Long says.

"Is there something we can do to stop him?" asks Alonzo.

"No, everything should be fine. I'll keep my eyes and ears open. It's just part of my job to deal with disappointed constituents," Long replies.

"Baton Rouge has the worst of them. Your guards should keep a close eye on him and everyone else here, Senator Long," says Nathan.

"Senator, we'd like to thank you for tonight's meeting with us," Alonzo says.

"The pleasure is all mine. I'd like to invite the four of you to stay until the special session is complete. We can meet again when I return," Long says.

"That would be great, Senator Long. Thank you for the invitation," Alonzo says.

"So, that settles it. You wait here for me. I'll be back soon. We are almost through the House process," Long says as he moves to the door. Long walks them out to the waiting area of the governor's office. "Margaret, I'll return from the House Chamber and continue my meeting with Alonzo later," Long says.

"I understand, Huey," says Margaret. "Have a seat and get comfortable, Alonzo. Senator Long will be done soon." Long's bodyguards quickly enter the governor's office and escort him out to the corridor.

The suspicious man, Dr. Carl Weiss, who's waiting outside the office door approaches Long once again. He says, "House Bill Number One is a mistake. You must reconsider, Senator Long."

Long's bodyguard, Bill Faquet intervenes. "Senator Long is not available to discuss the matter any further," he says as he pushes Weiss to the side. Long enters the House Chamber, opening the massive one ton bronze door leading to the lobby.

"Huey, we've been waiting for you to return. Let's head over to speak with Ellender," says Governor Allen. Long moves carefully through the crowd, observing their body language and searching for resistance to the bills. Long and Governor Allen walk toward House Speaker Allen Ellender who is waiting at his dais to meet with them about the proceedings.

"Huey, we've done all that we could. It's just a matter of time before the bills are passed," says Ellender.

"Everything has gone smoothly tonight," Governor Allen says. "I don't expect any further delay this evening."

"You have the full support of the House of

Representatives," Ellender says. A page approaches Ellender and hands him a notice. "Governor Allen and Senator Long, all 42 bills have now passed the House," says Ellender.

Long shakes Ellender's hand and smiles. He turns to speak with Governor Allen. "That was my kind of victory," says Long.

"Our work is done for the evening," says Governor Allen.

"Thank you for everything, Oscar," Long says. He turns down the center aisle of the House Chamber and walks out to the corridor. People begin to clap as Long arrives. Long's bodyguards walk just ahead of him down the hall.

Dr. Carl Weiss is now adamant about speaking with Senator Long. Weiss approaches Long just as he makes his way toward the governor's office. "Can I have a word with you, Senator?" asks Weiss. Long ignores him. "Hey, don't walk past me. I'm speaking to you," Weiss insists as he lunges toward Long.

"What's done is done," replies Long. Weiss suddenly pulls out a pistol.

Long's bodyguard, Harry Bozeman, jumps forward

to block Weiss' shot. "Stop!" yells Harry. Weiss shoots Senator Long in his abdomen.

Long shouts, "Why me?!! Help me please!" Long's bodyguards immediately attack Weiss with their machine guns and pistols, shooting him over 50 times. Blood flies wildly from Weiss' lifeless body and head. Weiss collapses to the floor in a pool of his blood. His shredded skin splashes violently to his feet. Long's bodyguards are merciless in their slaughter of Weiss. The crowd of bystanders in the corridor is mortified. Alonzo, Nathan, Louise and Ora are startled when they hear the barrage of gunshots, hoping prayerfully that Huey P. Long has not been harmed.

"Back up! Move away from the body!" shouts Long's bodyguards as they forcefully secure the area. Huey P. Long stumbles 40 feet down the capitol corridor to a flight of 28 steep stairs. He's loaded into the car of Samuel James.

"Where are you taking me?" asks Long gasping for breath.

"Our Lady of the Lake Hospital," replies Samuel as he helps the Senator find comfort in the car.

Long's bodyguards enter Governor Allen's office

and say, "Remain calm. Senator Long is still alive."
Everyone breathes a sigh of relief. Margaret Wright is in
tears. "I'm so worried about Huey. What happened?"
Margaret sobs.

Governor Allen enters his office surrounded by
bodyguards. The phones begin to ring repeatedly.
"Margaret, inform the press that Senator Long was injured
by an assassin, but that he's still alive and well," Allen says.

"Yes, Governor Allen. I'll answer the phones right
away and inform the press," says Margaret gathering
herself.

"Escort everyone out of the capitol building
immediately," Governor Allen commands the bodyguards.
Alonzo, Nathan, Louise and Ora enter the corridor and
view Dr. Carl Weiss' annihilated body on the bloody floor.
Ora is horrified. She's never seen a dead body destroyed so
violently. Long's bodyguards are shouting and running
feverishly through the halls of the capitol building. The
state police guard the House Chamber and the crowd
quickly moves out of the building. Once Alonzo, Nathan,
Louise and Ora exit the capitol building they are very
relieved. The tense atmosphere at the capitol is solemn.

"Ora, I'm so sorry. You must be very disappointed

about the shooting," says Alonzo.

"I'm very sorry too. Long is so close to you. I'm praying for Long's healing," Ora says.

"Try to calm down. We'll see you when you've had a chance to rest and you return to New Orleans," Alonzo says.

"Be careful on the River Road tonight. The encouraging thing is that Huey P. Long is still alive," Nathan says.

"This is the last thing I ever thought would happen to Long tonight. He was nearly invincible," Louise says.

"All men are vulnerable to attacks. Even Long was one shot away from fallibility," Alonzo says.

"Everything Long's worked for and his plans to run for president might have all been destroyed by one angry man," says Ora.

"That's just a part of life, Ora. Let's hope for the best," Nathan says.

"Ora and Nathan, we're headed back down to New Orleans now. Let's keep our heads held high in spite of tonight's attack," Alonzo says.

"Good night, Alonzo and Louise," says Ora as they walk over to their cars and leave the capitol.

"Ora, you never should have experienced this. I'm very upset about the shootings," Nathan says.

"Papa, I'm praying so hard. I never imagined that Long would actually be attacked," says Ora. Nathan and Ora climb into his car and Nathan turns the ignition on. Nathan piles into the bunch making its way out to North 3rd Street.

"Ora, I had a bad feeling about the evening when I saw the assassin approach Long in the corridor. Long's bodyguards should never have allowed the assassin to come anywhere near Long," Nathan says. He turns onto Scotland Avenue toward home. The traffic is frenzied due to the Long emergency. News has quickly spread that Huey P. Long has been attacked. Nathan pulls into his driveway and stops the car.

"Senator Long was so patient with the violent man who shot him. He was kind to the end," Ora says. Nathan and Ora climb out of the car and walk toward the house.

Ida is there waiting at the front door for them to arrive. "How was your meeting with Senator Long?" asks Ida.

"Ida, Senator Long was shot by an assassin," replies Nathan as he and Ora enter the house. Ida is terrified.

Nathan consoles Ida and walks her into the living room. Ora sits down next to Ida. "Where are the girls?" asks Nathan.

"They're asleep. It's been a difficult evening," replies Ida.

"Long is still alive, but he was rushed to the hospital for his wound," explains Nathan.

"Has the assassin been caught?" Ida asks.

"The assassin was killed instantly by Long's bodyguards," Nathan replies.

"The capitol building was evacuated after the shooting," Ora says.

"Were you ever able to meet with Long tonight?" Ida asks.

"Long met and spoke with us extensively," Ora replies. "Long was in such good spirits tonight."

"The assassin looked suspicious when he approached Long just as we arrived," says Nathan.

"This is all so strange. I don't understand how one man was able to get a gun past all of the security at the capitol building," says Ida.

"They never suspected that the man would be so dangerous. The mistake may have cost Huey P. Long his life and America its best president," Ora says.

"Ora, it's time for you to give your grandmothers a call before they hear the news about the attack," says Nathan. Ora walks over to the phone to call her grandmothers.

"Good evening. May I ask who's speaking?" Josephine asks.

"Ma Mere, it's Ora. How are you tonight?" Ora asks.

"We're all fine, sweetie. How was tonight's meeting with Senator Long?" asks Josephine.

"Ma Mere, Senator Long was attacked by an assassin at the capitol building while we were there waiting to meet with him a second time," replies Ora.

"How could this happen? He has so much security, Ora," Josephine says. She's silent for a moment.

"Are you alright, Ma Mere?" Ora asks.

"Is Senator Long still alive?" Josephine asks.

"Senator Long is still alive, Ma Mere. He was rushed to the hospital immediately," says Ora.

"We must go into serious prayer for Long," says Josephine.

"You're right. I'll have Papa, Ida and my sisters all

pray for Long together," Ora says.

"That's right, Ora. You can do it. I need to speak with your father if I can," says Josephine.

Ora says to Nathan, "Ma Mere would like to speak with you, Papa."

"I'm coming now," Nathan says as he walks over to the phone. "Good evening, Ma Mere."

"Hello, Nathan. Is Ora in any danger tonight?" asks Josephine.

"Ora is no longer in danger. We all made it safely out of the capitol building tonight with no injuries. The assassin was killed," replies Nathan.

"I'm very sorry that Senator Long was attacked. When will Ora return to New Orleans?" asks Josephine.

"Ora will return tomorrow afternoon," replies Nathan.

"I'm relieved to hear that she'll be back in the afternoon," says Josephine.

"Get some rest tonight and try not to worry, Ma Mere," Nathan says.

"Good night, Nathan," Josephine says. Nathan hands the phone back to Ora.

"Ma Mere, I'm so worried about Long," says Ora.

"Everything will be alright, even if heaven takes Senator Long home. God will make a way," says Josephine.

"I love you, Ma Mere," says Ora.

"I'll be waiting for you with a big meal when you arrive tomorrow," Josephine says.

"I can't wait to see you and Ma Mum. Good night, Ma Mere," Ora says.

"Good night," says Josephine.

"Ora, have a seat here with us," says Nathan. Ora walks over and takes a seat next to Ida.

"Ora, you're returning to New Orleans in the morning, but I'm still very concerned about your safety," says Nathan.

"Papa, I understand the dangers, but it might be safer in New Orleans now that Long's been attacked here in Baton Rouge," Ora says.

"Ora, the conditions in New Orleans will quickly worsen if Long actually passes," Nathan says. "Louisiana could face a major crisis if Long dies."

"Louisiana is completely dependent upon Huey P. Long," Ida says.

"We'll be devastated if we lose Long. Please pray

with me for Long," Ora says. Ora takes Nathan's and Ida's hands and begins to pray. "God, please heal and restore Huey P. Long. Please strengthen him and bless him," prays Ora.

"Ora, I'm proud of you for surviving the attack and praying," Nathan says.

"Having you there with me at the capitol helped to calm my fears," Ora says. Nathan embraces Ora. Ida gives Ora a hug.

"Good night, Ora. We'll see you in the morning," Nathan says. Ora walks down the hallway to the bathroom. She closes the door behind her and begins to finally cry. She's emotionally exhausted and very discouraged that the one leader who cared about their work for desegregation could soon die. Ora washes her tears away and takes a shower. She walks to her sister's room quietly so that she doesn't disturb them. Ora tip toes past her three sisters and sits down on her bed. Ora changes into her pajamas. She lies down and her mind begins to race. Ora thinks about how glad Walmsley will be to hear that Long has been shot. She thinks about the men in the White League and the Square Deal Association who have waited for Long to finally be attacked. Ora realizes that Louisiana needs Long so much to hold the state together peacefully. She thinks about segregation and Long's campaign for president. Ora begins to accept the possibility of Long's death and what it would mean for poor people and Black people and children who wouldn't otherwise have access to education. Ora takes comfort in knowing that men like Governor Allen will fight to preserve Long's legacy if he passes away. Ora begins to calm down and she eventually falls asleep as she thinks back to her final moments with Huey P. Long.

CHAPTER 6 / "MOURNING A LOSS"

The savory aroma of freshly prepared breakfast fills the morning air for Ora as she sulks in grief. Ora's body is weak, although she's alert and focused on the day ahead.

"Ora, would you like some scrambled eggs, biscuits and orange juice?" asks Ellis.

"Yes, Ma Mum. That would be nice," replies Ora. "I feel hungry, but I wouldn't have eaten if you hadn't cooked this morning."

"Ora, that's why we're up early for you this morning. We knew that you would be distracted,"

Josephine says.

"I'd like some breakfast, Ma Mum," says Cleo.

"So would I," says Alexia. Josephine serves
breakfast to them.

"Your breakfast is always so good, Ma Mum. It
really gets me going in the morning," Cleo says.

"When I was your age, we didn't have this kind of
meal in the mornings. We always had oatmeal or bread,"
reveals Ellis.

"Those were difficult days, but you made it
through," says Josephine.

"Just like you will make it through this day, Ora. It
may be tough, but God has so much in store for you," Ellis
says.

Ora sighs and says, "I trust you, Ma Mum. If I can
just make it through this day, I'll be alright."

"You can do it, Ora. Just say a prayer whenever you
feel discouraged. God will answer your prayers," Ellis says.

"I'll be in prayer throughout the day," Ora says.

"I'll even pray with you," says Ellis.

"Nathan and Alonzo should be here soon," says
Josephine.

"I just can't believe that Huey P. Long is actually

gone," Ellis says.

"I've been so down since the shooting. I can't forget how kind Long was to me," Ora says.

"Huey P. Long was one in a million," says Josephine.

"He truly was. Through the years I always thought of him as a distant star far out of reach. He turned out to be a very down to earth hands-on leader," Ora says.

"Long is in a better place now," says Alexia.

"It's so unfair that he had to die," Cleo says.

"Yes, Cleo, we have truly lost a great man," says Ellis.

"Long was more than just a great Senator or governor, he was a great person," says Josephine.

"The funeral should be very special for Long's family and the people of Louisiana," says Ora.

"Long's family lost him only two days ago. They must be so hurt. I wish that I could have met Long in person before he passed away," Josephine says.

"Meeting Long would have been a wonderful experience," says Ellis.

"There's so much that Long could have done, but Carl Weiss robbed him of the chance," says Ora.

"Louisiana will never be the same without Huey P. Long," Cleo says.

"I still look in the newspapers for stories on the work that Long's doing, not realizing that he's gone," Alexia says.

"You're coping with the loss a lot better than I am, Alexia," says Ora.

"Be encouraged and don't lose hope, Ora," Ellis says.

"Alonzo and Louise are keeping my spirits up by allowing me to cover Long's life," Ora shares.

"Alonzo has always known how to cover the key moments in our lives," says Josephine.

"Alonzo hasn't really been the same since Long passed away, but he's trying his best to stay focused," Ora says.

"Alonzo will get better soon, Ora. Just try to be patient with him," says Josephine. Alonzo knocks at the front door.

Ora walks over and answers the door. "Good morning, Alonzo. Please come in," she says.

"Good morning, Ora. How are you holding up today?" asks Alonzo.

"I'm doing a little better. I'm just trying to take it one step at a time," Ora replies.

"Good morning, Ellis and Josephine. How are you today?" asks Alonzo.

"We're alright. It's a long day ahead," replies Josephine.

"I'll be glad to spend the day with you, despite the somber occasion," says Alonzo.

"We should've gotten together sooner," Josephine says.

"Ora, Alexia and Cleo, come with me. Louise is in the car outside waiting," Alonzo says.

"Ellis and I will soon follow you when Nathan arrives," Josephine says.

"Goodbye, Ma Mum and Ma Mere. We'll see you in Baton Rouge at the capitol building," says Ora. They walk outside to his car and climb in. "Good morning, Louise," Ora says.

"Good morning Ora, Cleo and Alexia. It's good to see the three of you," Louise says.

"We have to hurry, because the crowds may be too large at the funeral for us to view the ceremony," says Alonzo.

"I hope that Papa makes it here soon to drive Ma Mum and Ma Mere to Baton Rouge as well," says Ora.

"I look forward to seeing Nathan there and at the house," says Alonzo.

"Papa has a lot to talk about with you. He's been very concerned since the shooting," Ora says.

"I know that Nathan has a lot on his mind. Baton Rouge is going to be a different place now that Long's gone," says Alonzo. He turns onto Claiborne Avenue toward Airline Highway.

"Nathan is probably frustrated by the assassination and the chaos in Baton Rouge," Louise says.

"Papa is so disappointed and he hasn't fully recovered from Long's death," says Ora.

"We've all been affected by Long's death in one way or another," Alonzo says.

"Papa is particularly concerned about Walmsley and the white supremacists now that Long's gone," Ora says.

"Nathan has every right to be concerned. They pose a major threat to Blacks throughout the state," Alonzo says.

"Papa is ready to continue covering segregation in Baton Rouge, although Long is no longer there," says Ora.

"We're certainly ready to encourage and support

Nathan's every effort," Louise says.

"There's so much work to be done to fight segregation. Long would have wanted us to make a major push in his honor," Alonzo says.

"Even now, we're in a position to fight for Walmsley's resignation," Ora urges.

"Ora, give me some time to prepare for a Walmsley confrontation. Timing is very important. Walmsley is likely fixated on Long's death right now," Alonzo explains. He drives through Metairie on Airline Highway. The traffic is heavy, because many people are traveling to the funeral.

"Everyone will be focused on Long for the next year, because he died so suddenly. His assassination was such a disappointment to the American people," says Louise.

"The national news coverage of Huey P. Long has been constant," says Alonzo.

"I'm not surprised that all of the schools are closed for the funeral, because it's a national tragedy," Louise says.

"The students just couldn't concentrate after the attack," says Alexia. "They were so upset."

"The students have been so discouraged by the

assassination. They'll never be another leader like Long,"
says Cleo.

"Long was so far ahead of his time that we'll never
catch up to his vision," Ora says.

"Don't give up hope, Ora. Even President Roosevelt
has been influenced by Long and he won't forget his
message," Alonzo says.

"I just don't believe that President Roosevelt is very
committed to desegregation in the South," says Ora.

"President Roosevelt will never have the same
understanding as Long, but he has made some efforts for
Black people," Louise says.

"It will be interesting to see how President
Roosevelt reacts to Long's assassination," says Alonzo.

"President Roosevelt is probably very disappointed
to lose a leading Democrat," says Ora.

"'Long's death is a huge loss for the Democratic
Party. Long organized millions of supporters for the party,"
Louise says.

"President Roosevelt's reelection could be credited
to Long, because he generated so much interest for the
Democratic Party," says Alonzo.

"Long changed the Democratic Party forever with

his Share Our Wealth activism," Ora says.

"Long supported Roosevelt for president in 1932, but he soon decided to oppose him," says Alonzo.

"Long pushed Roosevelt to adopt the Revenue Act of 1935, raising income taxes to the levels he proposed in his Share Our Wealth bills," Louise says.

"It's unbelievable that Long was able to convince Roosevelt to adopt the Revenue Act despite their many differences," Ora says.

"The Revenue Act was one of Long's final victories, because it was enacted on August 30th, only thirteen days before he passed away," says Louise.

"Only time will tell how important the Revenue Act will be to raise the needed funding to support Roosevelt's New Deal social programs," Alonzo says.

"The American people will have Huey P. Long to thank for many years to come,'" says Ora.

"We certainly will, Ora," says Alonzo.

"I wish that I could view Long's body up close, but I know that it's almost impossible," says Cleo.

"The crowd will be overwhelming at the capitol, but it's important for us to be there today," says Alexia.

"I would have loved to have introduced you to

Long, because he was so personable," Ora says.

"I'm sorry we missed the opportunity. I'll always remember how excited you were to meet him," Cleo says.

"Senator Long really changed our lives for the better. I'll never forget the work that he's done," Alexia says.

"Every major highway, bridge, road, hospital and state building was constructed as a result of the Long administration. He transformed the Louisiana school system," says Ora.

"Long should also be remembered for his stance against big oil companies in Louisiana," says Alonzo.

"Long's tax on the production of refined oil funds most of his many improvements. The tax changes so much for the people of Louisiana," Louise says.

"Former Governor John Parker who plotted Long's assassination with Walmsley despised Long for his outspoken stance against oil companies. Long actually supported Parker's run for governor in 1920, but he later realized that Parker failed to take a stand against corporate interest and oil companies," Alonzo shares.

"Long tried so hard to fight white supremacists when he ran against Parker for governor in 1924, but he didn't have the needed support," Louise says.

"When Long was elected governor in 1928, he accomplished so much more for the state than any previous governor," Alonzo says.

"The Kingfish was truly an original," Ora says.

"Long held on tightly to the governorship even when he was elected Senator," Alonzo says.

"Long ran for the Senate in an effort to rebuild momentum for his key construction proposals," Louise says. "He even promised to resign if he was defeated by Joseph Ransdell."

"We risked losing Long to a bold promise, but Long delivered once again," Ora says.

"Long rarely came up short. He would probably still be alive if he'd received the care he needed to recover," says Alonzo.

"He was very animated in the hospital after the shooting," Louise says laughing.

"He was a fighter until the end. Long's legacy is one of victory over poverty for Louisiana," Ora says.

"You're right, Ora. Long will always be remembered for enriching the state despite the criticisms of his opponents," Alonzo says.

"Why didn't Long receive the best care available and survive, Alonzo?" asks Alexia.

"The doctors Long needed were based in New Orleans and they had a hard time traveling to Baton Rouge," replies Alonzo.

"How could one gunshot wound kill a man as powerful as Long?" Cleo asks.

"The odds were against Long despite all that he'd done to improve healthcare in Louisiana," Alonzo replies.

"The doctors underestimated the severity of Long's injuries, because he was so active at the hospital," Louise says.

"The doctors will never be able to forget their mistakes, because they were so costly," Ora says.

"The hospital will never make this kind of mistake again now that Long's gone," Alonzo says. Alonzo drives through Gonzales toward Baton Rouge. The traffic is gradually building and the people are moving rapidly toward the capitol city.

"Long's family must be devastated. They had no way to prepare for Long to die this way," Louise says.

"Long's family has been in my prayers since the night of the shooting," says Ora.

"What did it feel like to be there at the capitol on the night of the shooting?" asks Cleo.

"The shooting was unreal. I've never seen so much blood," Ora says.

"I wouldn't have been able to keep myself together if I had been there that night," Alexia says.

"It all happened so quickly. We didn't actually see Long's gunshot wound," Ora says.

"It was so tough for Long to walk out of the capitol building on his own," Cleo says.

"When we heard the gunshots, I knew that Long had been hit. I had an eerie feeling that Long wouldn't make it," Louise says.

"I was confident that Long could survive the shooting that night. Long had never given in, even under the worst circumstances," Alonzo says.

"Long's will to live did not fail. He nearly defeated death," Ora says.

"The assassination was one of the first of a presidential candidate," Cleo says.

"Of all the people who plotted to kill Long, Carl Weiss was the least likely to pull the trigger," Alonzo says.

"That's why Weiss was so easily able to gain access

to Long. He was so unassuming," Louise says.

"When I noticed Carl Weiss for the first time at the capitol building, he seemed to be in distress. I never imagined that he would murder Senator Long," Ora says.

"Long has so many different kinds of enemies. Weiss was the intelligent calculating type of assassin, the most dangerous type of them all," Alonzo says.

"Some people suspect that Weiss didn't actually shoot Long. Rumors are swirling about an accidental shooting by Long's bodyguards who reacted to Weiss' threatening movements," Louise says.

"The rumors are just plain wrong. Long's bodyguards would have never shot him accidentally. Long trained his men so well that they were prepared for just about anything," Alonzo insists.

"Long's bodyguards were so focused that night. Their only mistake was to let Carl Weiss come anywhere near Long," Ora says.

"What type of person was Carl Weiss?" asks Cleo.

"Weiss was very nervous and aggressive with Long. He appeared to be angry with the Senator," Alonzo says.

"Weiss didn't give in even when Long responded to him. Weiss pushed his way to the Senator and wouldn't back down," says Louise.

"We were in the governor's office when Weiss approached Long for the last time. Long vaguely mentioned Weiss and House Bill Number One during our meeting," Ora says.

"Long felt that something was wrong when he met with us, but he dealt with Weiss as though he was harmless," Louise says.

"If Long realized just how dangerous Weiss really was, he would have stopped him immediately," Ora says.

"The assassination was inevitable," Cleo says.

"Long's life was in his own hands that night. Long was just too tolerant," says Alexia.

"I should have alerted Long to my suspicions of Weiss," Louise says.

"Long might have listened to you if you'd warned him, Louise," Ora says.

"If Long's bodyguards had just known to search Weiss for his gun, Long would still be alive today," says Alonzo.

"So much more could have been done for Long, but everyone let down their guard at the wrong time," Louise says. Alonzo arrives in Baton Rouge and drives toward the capitol.

"We made it to Baton Rouge just in time," says Louise. There are thousands of people in attendance at Long's funeral. It's difficult for Alonzo to enter the capitol grounds, because there's such high security and so many vehicles in the surrounding area. They are an hour early for the funeral, so Alonzo is able to find an area to park further down on North 3rd Street. The police guide the cars into the open lot and monitor the traffic.

Alonzo parks his car in the back corner of the lot, so that he won't attract attention to himself as a Black person. They climb out of the car and walk toward the capitol building. Alonzo says, "We're not too far away. We still have a lot of time before the funeral begins." They see people from all walks of life make their way to Long's funeral. Ora begins to wonder if the people realize how close Long came to immortality. She thinks about the night of the shooting and how vigilant Long's bodyguards were. She considers what would have happened if Long's bodyguards had blocked Weiss' approach. She dreams of an event celebrating Long's life instead of a massive funeral commemorating Long today. Alonzo interrupts Ora's racing thoughts by asking, "Are you ready for the grueling day ahead?"

"I'm thinking about Long a lot and I wish that he was waiting here at the capitol for us to arrive," Ora replies.

"Long is here. He just can't reach out to shake your hand again," Alonzo says. He gives Ora a small hug and Louise pats Ora on her back. She begins to cry a little, but she wipes her tears away quietly.

Alexia consoles Ora and says, "You'll feel better once the funeral begins."

"Being here at the funeral will help you realize how many people care about Long and appreciate him," Cleo says.

"Alexia and Cleo, thank you. Having you here today makes me feel so much better," says Ora. The five of them make it to the capitol building and the grounds are completely transformed. Long's final resting place is prepared in the capitol gardens lined with hundreds of funeral wreaths. Thousands of people are gathered on the capitol walkways waiting for the ceremonies to begin. Louise photographs the ceremony's early moments with her camera. She captures the pain of the many people through her small lens. She focuses in on the families with tears and their impressions of the massive crowd. Louise photographs several small children and highlights their youth among the onslaught of adults. She takes snapshots of Alonzo, Ora, Cleo and Alexia as they experience the moment. Louise takes pictures of the capitol building itself with the crowd filling its entrances. She stops to save her film for the ceremony to begin.

Alonzo sees Nathan arrive with Josephine and Ellis. "I'm so glad you made it in time before the crowds grew too large," says Alonzo.

Nathan hugs Ora and Alexia. "Hi girls. It's good to finally be here," says Nathan.

"Hi, Papa. Hi, Ma Mere and Ma Mum," says Ora.

"Hi, Ora. I don't think I've ever seen so many people attend a funeral before" says Josephine.

"Huey P. Long was as popular as a president," Ellis says.

"There would have been many more people here if they'd delayed the funeral for another week," Ora says.

"They wanted to keep the numbers low to manage the crowd," Josephine says. The ceremonies begin with a viewing of Long's body. The large procession of people march slowly through the capitol rotunda.

"We should get in line to view Long's body,"

Alonzo says.

"You're right, Alonzo. This will be the last chance for everyone to see the Senator," Nathan says. They all make their way to the end of the line and patiently wait to see Long for the last time.

"It will be very interesting to finally see Long in person," Cleo says.

"Long's ghost will haunt his opponents," Alexia says.

"I've been haunted by Carl Weiss since the night of the attack," Louise says.

"Ma Mum and Ma Mere, we've been talking a lot about the shooting on the way to Baton Rouge," Ora says.

"We have too. The shooting will be on everyone's mind for a long time, but you should remember that Long would have wanted us to focus on his vision for the country," Josephine says.

"Ma Mum, can you withstand the hours on your feet out here?" asks Alexia.

"Ma Mum, I can bring the car here to you if you feel too tired to continue," Nathan says.

"Thank you, Nathan. I'll let you know if I need help," says Ellis. They all move closer to the capitol building as the line progresses. Louise photographs some of the people in the procession. There are a good number of Black people in attendance that surprises Josephine and Ellis. Blacks are not discouraged from viewing Long's body.

As Alonzo, Louise, Ora and her family enter the rotunda they begin to experience the grandeur of the event. Huey P. Long is lain in a bronze open double casket with copper lining covered with glass. His body is outfitted in a black tuxedo, white pleated shirt and tie. State police guard Long's body formally armed with rifles. Alonzo and Louise view Long's body first followed by Nathan, Josephine and Ellis. Ora, Alexia and Cleo follow them into the capitol building. Louise photographs the rotunda and Long's casket. Lavish wreaths surround Huey P. Long and the rotunda is ornately decorated.

When Ora views Senator Long, chills run through her body. She can't accept Long's death after seeing him alive and well. She looks down at Long's cold face and realizes that her journey has just begun. Ora sees the pain in Long's death and she begins to understand how much work needs to be done in Long's absence. She internalizes Long's fight against white supremacists. She begins to understand just how hard Long worked to shield Black people from the very worst violence and hatred in Louisiana. At this moment, Ora is inspired to not only fight Mayor Walmsley, but to fight segregation throughout the nation many years after Walmsley is voted out or put out of office. Ora thinks back to the treasured moments that she spent with Huey P. Long and she accepts the responsibility that she has as a privileged journalist to fight segregation with the same commitment demonstrated by the slain Senator. As Ora says goodbye to Senator Long for the last time, she's overcome with admiration and appreciation for a man who literally gave his life for the people of America at a time when few men had the courage to fight at all. At this moment, Ora relinquishes fear and dedicates her life to the fight against segregation and the chains of poverty that Long broke through during his celebrated life.

"You look like you might make it through the day," Alonzo says.

"Seeing Huey P. Long one last time has changed my way of thinking," Ora says.

"What do you mean, Ora?" asks Alonzo.

"Long gave his life to the people of Louisiana and stood up for those who never had a voice. Long has inspired my life in a way now that he's lost his. I'll never forget his strength," replies Ora.

"I knew that attending the funeral together would be very meaningful for you, Ora," says Alonzo.

"These moments with Long are just as special as the time he gave to us alive," Ora says.

"I'm very encouraged to hear your inspired words about the Senator," Alonzo says.

"Long has given you a very important gift. You will do great things in his honor," says Josephine.

"I felt something very special when I viewed Long's body like his spirit was right there watching over us," says Ellis.

"I feel Long's powerful spirit too. He was a blessing to so many people," says Josephine. They walk out to the capitol gardens to the interment site. There is a large crowd gathered there waiting for Reverend Gerald L. K. Smith to lead the procession of Long's body to the interment. They watch as Long's body is marched from the capitol building to the capitol gardens. The march is slow and prayerful. The crowd is silent as the procession continues. Ora begins to cry again as she watches Long become one with the capitol that he painstakingly built. Josephine embraces Ora and comforts her. Alexia also begins to cry. Ellis wipes her tears away. With each step taken by the procession, Ora's heart begins to pound forcefully. She holds on to every moment of the solemn occasion. Once the procession arrives at the burial site, Long's body reaches his wife, Rose, his sons Russell and Palmer and his daughter Rose. Long's brothers Earl and George are there waiting with Long's widow.

Reverend Smith begins to eulogize Long. He prays and says, "God is shining his light brightly upon the soul of Huey P. Long. He was not only a great man, but he was a compassionate man who gave everything he could to the people of Louisiana. Senator Long was a bright light in a world filled with darkness and hatred. Never before has a governor done so much for the people of Louisiana. His life was taken so suddenly from us all. It matter not how striked the gates, how charged with punishment the scroll. I am the master of my fate. I am the captain of my soul," says Reverend Smith. He lifts his hands in prayer. Everyone bows their heads to pray. Soldiers fire a 21-gun salute in honor of Senator Huey P. Long. The interment of Long's body begins. Governor Allen places the American flag on Long's closed casket. Long's wife, who is visibly shaken, places a dozen red roses on his casket.

"The funeral has brought closure to the very violent assassination," says Ora.

"I feel much better about Long's death now that I've seen the overwhelming support from people at the funeral," says Alonzo.

"I feel blessed just to be here," says Josephine.

"Nathan, thank you for making it possible for us to be here today," says Ellis.

"I'm glad that I was able to drive you to the funeral. It was important for you to be here with Ora. Everyone, please join us for dinner at our house. Ida has prepared a meal for us all," Nathan says.

"I'd be so glad to stop by," says Alonzo.

"We should hurry before the people crowd the streets and make it impossible to leave," Nathan says. Everyone walks to the parking lots and returns to their cars. They climb into Alonzo's car and he turns the ignition on. He is able to slowly drive onto North 3rd Street through traffic. He drives toward Scotland Avenue and slowly makes it to Nathan's house. Nathan, Josephine and Ellis are there when Alonzo arrives. Nathan walks Josephine and Ellis to the front door.

Ida opens the front door for Nathan. She says, "You made it back just in time for dinner. Good evening Ellis and Josephine. How was the funeral?"

"The funeral was unlike anything I've experienced. There were tens of thousands of people in attendance," replies Nathan.

"I'm really glad to hear that the people were there to support Senator Long," Ida says.

"The funeral was a very moving experience for me," Ora says.

"I would have loved to have met Senator Long when he was alive. I just couldn't find the strength to attend the funeral," Ida says.

"The funeral would have encouraged you, because it was so special," Ora says.

"You're probably right, but I'll just have to settle for the news coverage of the funeral in the morning," Ida says. "Please come in and have a seat at the dining room table." Nathan helps Ellis and Josephine to their seats. "I have prepared basil roasted lamb, sweet potatoes, collard greens and stuffed crab for dinner tonight," says Ida. She begins to serve the meal with the help of Ora and Alexia.

"The food is much better than expected after the day

we've had," Nathan says laughing.

"Thank you so much for preparing the meal for us all," says Alonzo.

"You knew exactly what to prepare to make us feel better about the day," Ora says.

"I love you, Ida," Alexia says.

"I love you too, Ida," says Cleo.

"Alexia, Cleo and Ora, you know that I love you too. I'm just so glad that you're here tonight," says Ida.

"Having all of you with me has helped me to cope with the loss of Huey P. Long," Alonzo says.

"I feel the same way. I would be so lost without everyone's support during this difficult time," Nathan says.

"Were you able to view Long's body?" asks Ida.

"We all had a chance to view the body," replies Alonzo.

"I felt something spiritual when I was in Long's presence," says Josephine.

"Long's spirit is anointed even in death," Ellis says.

"Long has always had a powerful spirit. Death cannot defeat his memory," Ida says. Ora helps to clear the table when everyone finishes their meals.

"Come into the living room," Nathan says.

Josephine and Ellis sit down next to Nathan. Ora, Cleo and Alexia follow their grandmothers. Nathan begins to share old photographs of them with Alonzo and Louise.

Alonzo is pleasantly surprised to see the pictures. "Ora looks so much like her mother in the photographs," Alonzo says.

"Ora always did have a close resemblance to Cecilia. I'm so proud of them and how well they're doing in school," says Nathan.

"I always knew that Ora would be a writer. When the *Times Picayune* published her story 'The First Christmas' in 1927 I realized that Ora had a gift," says Josephine.

"Alexia and Cleo looked so much alike when they were children," Alonzo says.

"They have a distinct look of their own," Nathan says.

"Cleo is also a strong writer, but his gift is really artwork," says Nathan.

"I would be interested in seeing some of your artwork," Alonzo says.

"I'll have Ora send one of my paintings to your office soon," Cleo says.

"I would have liked to have known the three of you when you were children," Louise says.

"It certainly would have been nice to know you back then, Louise," says Ora.

"They were very special kids growing up. I remember them reading a lot and being unusually creative," says Nathan.

"I've always enjoyed Ora's writing. The City Hall incident was a turning point for me to realize that it was time for Ora to be published," Alonzo says.

"What made you decide to introduce Ora to Huey P. Long?" Nathan asks Alonzo.

"Long was eager to meet Ora after the City Hall shooting. He was pretty impressed by what he'd heard about Ora," replies Alonzo.

"Did you ever imagine that Ora would become the kind of writer who Long would want to meet?" asks Nathan.

"I'd never thought about Ora in the context of Long, because she'd never written any letters on him," replies Alonzo.

"Ora was so focused on Walmsley that she rarely thought about the many good things done by Long,"

Nathan says.

"Ora would have flourished under Long's Senate term and certainly under Long's presidency," Alonzo says.

"Long might have considered Ora for many different government positions," says Nathan.

"We were all so close to doing so much more with Long alive, but we'll pick up the pieces somehow," Alonzo says.

"Would you like some cake and coffee for dessert?" offers Ida. The group moves back to the dining room table as Ida walks over to the kitchen. Ora and Alexia help Ida serve the treat.

"We have a lot of work ahead," Alonzo says.

"I'm definitely ready to get started," Ora says.

"I hope you're ready to continue writing about segregation in Baton Rouge, Nathan," Alonzo says.

"That's the way Long would have wanted it," Louise says.

"Governor Allen will work to stabilize Baton Rouge, but the Square Deal Association will probably begin to organize resistance," Alonzo says.

"The state can survive, because Long selected his successor so far in advance of his death. The people really have a chance to recover," Nathan says.

"Governor Allen actually planned to succeed Long as Senator once he was able to win the presidency," Ora says.

"We're fortunate to have Governor Allen. He's just as kind as Long," Josephine says.

"If something were to happen to Governor Allen, we would be lost," Nathan says.

"I don't know, Nathan. Long groomed a lot of young leaders. Someone would pick up the torch," says Alonzo.

"You're right, Alonzo. A lot of young men who closely followed Long are eager to have a chance to lead. Long planted so many seeds," Nathan says.

"Long gave them so much to emulate. If they follow Long's lead, they'll certainly have the support of the people," Alonzo says.

"The lessons taught by Long are enduring. His legacy is rich and his young leaders are ready to fulfill his vision," says Nathan.

"I'd like to see one of Long's leaders oppose Walmsley for the mayoral position. We can definitely support that type of effort," Alonzo says.

"That's an excellent idea," says Louise.

"Having someone to compete for the mayor's position will disarm Walmsley and make him think twice about his abuse of Black people," Alonzo says.

"If you approach Walmsley from the political standpoint and lobby for his resignation, you'd have the support of the people," Nathan says.

"I'll work with Long's organization in New Orleans, generate support for a new candidate for mayor and commit to cover their campaign," Alonzo says.

"That's it, Alonzo. I know how hard it is for you to confront Walmsley, but this approach is better," says Nathan.

"Nathan, it's getting pretty late. We should head back to New Orleans soon," says Josephine.

"I'm glad to have been able to share a meal with everyone," says Ida.

"Ida and Nathan, thank you very much for dinner," says Alonzo. Ora and Alexia clear the dining room table.

"I wish that Ora, Cleo and Alexia could visit more often," says Josephine.

"I'll try to have the three of them here during the holidays," Nathan says. Alexia, Ora and Cleo hug Ida and

Nathan good night.

"Good night, Nathan and Ida. I hope to see you again soon," says Alonzo as he heads outside to his car with Cleo, Alexia and Ora. Nathan helps Josephine and Ellis to his car outside. They all climb into the cars and drive down to Scotland Avenue toward Airline Highway.

"Ora, we will cover today's funeral in next week's issue of the paper," Alonzo says.

"I should have some very nice photographs for the coverage," Louise says.

"I'd like to write an article on my experience of having met Long and lost him," Ora says.

"That would be a very interesting article," says Louise.

"I'd like to continue covering Long throughout the month of September," Alonzo says.

"Are you prepared to begin covering segregation and Walmsley again soon?" asks Ora.

"You will know when the time is right to cover Walmsley again, because he'll give us the story we need to send the right message," replies Alonzo.

"Walmsley is probably celebrating Long's death," Ora says.

"Walmsley can celebrate, but he'll suffer the consequences of Long's death in the end," Alonzo says.

"Walmsley will likely do the things that Long worked so hard to prevent him from doing," says Louise.

"Walmsley is capable of just about anything right now and only Governor Allen is there to stop him," Alonzo says.

"I'm ready to take on Walmsley despite his attacks," says Ora.

"Be patient, Ora. Wait for the right moment to confront Walmsley. I'd like you to cover racial disparities in the New Orleans school system and education," Alonzo says.

"That is a very important topic. You'll set yourself apart as a journalist when you cover the story," Louise says.

"I'm up to the challenge," says Ora.

"Long's work with education in Louisiana had a major impact on Black public schools, but there's still so much work to be done. I know that you cannot fully study segregated white schools to make a thorough comparison, but you can review the conditions of Black public schools in the city," Alonzo says.

"I can cover my school, McDonogh 35, interviewing our teachers and staff," says Ora.

"McDonogh 35 is a really good school," says Cleo.

"Even the best Black schools simply don't have the resources given to white schools," says Alonzo.

"I'm proud of McDonogh 35," Alexia says.

"Our schools are better than many other schools, but I know there's room for improvement," Ora says.

"Huey P. Long often discussed the inequality in the schools during his campaign. Long hoped to do much more for the schools than he could," says Alonzo.

"Long was very focused on education. Improvements were his priority," says Louise.

"When Long had the state to provide free textbooks to public and private schools, he made it so much better for families in need," says Ora.

"If Long were still alive, he would be planning a new program for the schools that would turn things around for Black students," says Cleo.

"I'd like you to cover the physical conditions of the schools, the drop-out rates, the graduation rates and the college entrance rates," Alonzo says.

"You'll need to do a lot of research, Ora," Louise

says.

"I can handle the story. The McDonogh 35 staff is very sharp," Ora says.

"You can take your time writing the article, because I'm in no rush. It's a long-term project," says Alonzo. He drives through LaPlace within minutes of New Orleans.

Ora begins to think about how different life will be without Huey P. Long. She thinks of New Orleans and the culture of the city. She thinks about the Black community and its rich heritage despite segregation. Ora wonders if Alonzo and Louise realize how important it is for them to take a stand against Walmsley. "Are you prepared for Walmsley to make an unprovoked move against you, Alonzo?" asks Ora.

"I'm not ready for harassment from Walmsley. I'll do what I can to avoid him until the time is right," replies Alonzo.

"When did you first begin to notice hostility from Walmsley?" asks Cleo.

"Walmsley heavily criticized Long and he had his men follow Long during Walmsley's campaign for reelection," replies Alonzo.

"Walmsley was very intimidated by Long," says

Ora.

"Long supported Walmsley's opponent John Klorer in the mayoral campaign after aligning with Walmsley briefly," says Alonzo.

"Walmsley suspects everyone who actively supports Long. Alonzo is on Walmsley's short list of journalists to attack," Louise says.

"How are you able to maintain a thriving newspaper with Walmsley's attacks?" asks Cleo.

"Long was always there to stop Walmsley when he was too aggressive. Long stripped Walmsley of most of his financial powers through the legislature and Long's guards patrolled the city carefully," replies Alonzo.

"Now we'll see just how evil Walmsley really is," Ora says.

"Walmsley's not completely free. He must answer to the people," Louise says.

Alonzo arrives in New Orleans and turns onto Claiborne Avenue. "Ora, I expect to see you tomorrow after school for our issue release," Alonzo says.

"I'll be there. I'm ready for the next chapter in the history of the state," Ora says.

"You're really encouraging me to move on, Ora,"

Louise says.

"You two have given me so much to look forward to despite Long's assassination," Ora says.

"I enjoyed having you with us today, Alexia and Cleo," says Alonzo.

"The day turned out better than expected," says Alexia.

"You're right, Alexia. I was so glad to see the large turnout at the funeral. Long's opponents discouraged me a lot, but now I know how much people loved Huey P. Long," Cleo says.

"Long has millions of supporters across the country. He'll always be remembered for his dedication," Ora says. Alonzo pulls up to the curb of Ora's house.

"Good night, Alonzo and Louise. Thank you for the ride to Baton Rouge," Ora says.

"Good night Ora, Cleo and Alexia," says Alonzo. They walk to the front door and enter the house.

Josephine and Ellis are there awaiting their arrival. "I'm relieved that you made it home," Josephine says.

"Good night, Ma Mere and Ma Mum," Ora says. She walks down the hallway to her bedroom. She gathers her pajamas from her dresser, then walks to the bathroom.

Ora takes a shower and brushes her teeth. She returns to the bedroom and puts her clothes away.

"Alonzo is taking Long's death pretty hard," Alexia says.

"Alonzo put a lot of hope into Huey P. Long. I now realize that he was able to look beyond the confines of segregation, because of Long," Ora says.

"Alonzo could really make a difference if he stands up to Walmsley," Alexia says.

"I tried to convince Alonzo to confront Walmsley for a year, but he's been so discouraged," Ora says.

"It doesn't help that Walmsley nearly had Alonzo arrested," mentions Alexia.

"Alonzo may never actually confront Walmsley again now that Long is gone," says Ora.

"It's alright for Alonzo to avoid Walmsley, because there's not much he can do on his own without Long," Alexia says.

"Alonzo is capable of much more than he realizes. He has the power to change the City of New Orleans," Ora says.

"You're dreaming, Ora. Alonzo just can't stand up to Walmsley," Alexia says.

"I promise you that by this time next year Walmsley will be gone," Ora says.

Alexia laughs and says, "Ora, if you're right, I'll be overjoyed."

"Get ready for a miracle. When Alonzo decides to get rid of Walmsley, he'll never look back," Ora says.

"I love you, Ora. I can't imagine what life would be without you," Alexia says.

"I love you too, Alexia," Ora says as she turns down the flame in her lantern.

"Good night, Ora," Alexia says. They both fall asleep quietly.

CHAPTER 7 / "THE COURAGEOUS STAND"

Alonzo Willis knocks at Ora Lewis' front door. Ora answers the door. "Are you ready for the protest?" asks Alonzo.

"I was born ready," replies Ora.

"Good morning, Ellis and Josephine," says Alonzo raising his right hand and waving. Cleo carries their picketing signs to the front door. Alexia helps Cleo with the signs.

"Let's head to the office and prepare for the protesters to arrive," says Alonzo. They all walk out to

Alonzo's car. Alonzo opens the trunk for Cleo to load the signs with the help of Alexia. They climb into the car and take off. Alonzo turns onto Claiborne Avenue toward Howard Avenue. "Ora, I'm very proud of you for organizing the protest. It was long overdue," says Alonzo.

"Mayor Walmsley has pushed us all too far. We couldn't sit in silence one more day," says Josephine.

"Alonzo, thank you for supporting the protest. It couldn't have happened without you," Ora says. Alonzo turns left onto Pine Street toward Washington Avenue.

"How many people will take part in the protest today?" asks Cleo.

"We're expecting over five hundred people," replies Ora.

"I don't even recognize you anymore, Ora, because you're so strong now," says Alexia.

"My life has changed completely and I feel like a new person inside," Ora says.

"I've lived for this moment in history when Ora would finally become a desegregation leader," says Josephine. Alonzo pulls into his driveway and there are cars parked all along the streets. There is a massive crowd gathered at the front door of Alonzo's office holding signs and waiting for the protest to begin.

When the crowd notices that they've arrived, the people begin to cheer for Ora and Alonzo. As they make their way to the front door of the office, the crowd makes room for them ahead. Louise and Nathan are there waiting for Alonzo and Ora to arrive. Louise has managed the crowd and prepared them for the grueling day ahead. She photographs the people.

Alonzo makes room for Ora at the front door. He turns to the crowd and says, "Good morning everyone. We are so honored that you have decided to join the protest today. Each of you is a leader in your own right. The decision to stand up for what is right is often a very difficult decision to make. The risks that you will take today are grave. We will all risk our freedom and we might all be arrested. Just remember that your visible demonstration of courage will not go unnoticed by the people of the City of New Orleans. We have been gathered here today by our own young writer, Ora Lewis and her message of hope has been received. Not only do we welcome Ora to the Sepia Socialite as a full-fledged member of our staff as a full-time writer, but we celebrate Ora as the leader of this powerful protest. I would now like to introduce Ora Lewis." Everyone in the crowd applauds.

Ora turns to the crowd and says, "How wonderful it is to look out to your many faces and see the expression of determination. We have not been destroyed as a community. Jim Crow segregation has not erased our enduring sense of self. You have not been discouraged by the lack of coverage of the continuous abuse of Black people in the city. As you stand with me here today, I am reminded of the strength of our ancestors to fight racism, lynchings and slavery for centuries. We've come this far by faith, and no one can stop us from believing in the justice that has been promised us by emancipation. Your presence here today is living proof of our strength as a people to fight unceasingly for peace and freedom. We lost Senator Huey P. Long and we lost Governor Oscar Allen too soon, but we haven't lost our faith. Mayor Walmsley has attacked us without mercy since Senator Long's assassination. He has had many of us arrested, murdered, hunted down and intimidated for voting and for little else than moving freely throughout the city. This type of harassment must come to an end. In our protest today, we will stand before City Hall and peacefully demonstrate in an effort to stop Mayor Walmsley. He will resign, because the City of New Orleans is in financial crisis. The city has nearly collapsed as a result of the mayor's total loss of power. Mayor Walmsley is not invincible. He can be stopped. We will stop his attacks and we will bring an end to his destruction of the city starting today with our protest and for every difficult day ahead. When we protest today at City Hall, let us not turn to the right or turn to the left in fear, but let us press forward in hope of delivering the city from its depression and despair. We are not insignificant victims of Walmsley's attacks. We are survivors who will live to see the day when the city is restored and set free. Let us now gather on the steps of Gallier Hall and send a message loud and clear to Mayor Walmsley and to the city that we will not give in until he resigns. We have waited patiently for this day and we will not turn back until the protest is recorded on the pages of history today and for all generations to come." The crowd applauds Ora's words of inspiration.

Alonzo steps to the forefront and addresses the crowd. "Thank you, Ora. You have inspired us all. Everyone, let's head to Gallier Hall and begin protesting. We will see you there," says Alonzo. The crowd claps and disperses. The large group packs into their cars and heads to the protest.

Ora gathers with Alonzo and Louise in the office. She says, "Thank you for welcoming me to the staff of the Sepia Socialite as a full-time writer, Alonzo."

"You deserve the position after all that you've done for the paper and the community," says Alonzo.

"Congratulations, Ora," says Louise.

"Alonzo, thank you for hiring Ora," says Josephine.

"We should prepare to leave for City Hall right away," Alonzo says. He secures the office doors and walks to his car with Louise and Ora. Cleo, Alexia, Josephine and Ellis ride with Nathan to City Hall. Alonzo drives toward Carrollton Avenue from Erato Street, following the long line of cars from the gathering.

"I didn't realize how effective I'd become until this morning when I saw the crowd," says Ora.

"The people were very moved by your effort to organize the protest. I've never seen the community so encouraged about desegregation," Louise says.

"I'm confident that Walmsley will be seriously influenced by today's protest. There's no way for him to prepare for the attention generated by such a large crowd," Alonzo says.

"Walmsley may immediately react to the protest

with a police standoff," says Louise.

"Walmsley's men are my biggest concern, because they can do more damage than the police," Alonzo says.

"Walmsley's men may actually hide from plain view," suggests Louise.

"I won't be surprised if Walmsley's men show up today and threaten us once Walmsley realizes that the protest has begun," Ora says.

"Ora, you should be prepared for anything to happen," Alonzo says. He turns onto Poydras Street from Claiborne Avenue and drives toward City Hall.

"The people have been through so much from Walmsley that they're prepared for the worst," Ora says.

"People expect Walmsley to attack them and harass them, because he's done it so often," reasons Louise.

"I'll watch for any signs of withdrawal from the crowd once Walmsley begins his attacks," says Alonzo.

"The protesters will probably begin strong, but they will quickly lose strength if the attacks begin," Louise says.

"I can see a different result altogether, because Walmsley will not be able to break the backs of the people," Ora says.

"Ora, you may be right and I certainly hope you

are," says Louise.

"Ora, the people have the will to make it through the protest. They have to make the decision to stay and fight," Alonzo says. He arrives at City Hall and many of the protesters have begun to gather in Lafayette Square. Alonzo parks his car on Girod Street and they walk back to Saint Charles Avenue.

"I'm proud to be a part of your protest, Ora," says Louise.

"I still can't believe that the protest is actually happening today. Look at the crowd and realize that God has inspired the people to finally confront Mayor Walmsley together as one," Ora says. The protesters hold up their signs that read "Mayor Walmsley, We Are Free" and "Stop The Attacks." Alonzo, Louise and Ora walk over to the steps of City Hall taking their places at the front of the crowd. Alonzo and Ora turn to the crowd of over five hundred people and raise their hands in jubilation. Reporters and photographers from the *Times Picayune* and the *New Orleans Item* begin to take photos of the protesters. Louise photographs Alonzo, Ora and the protesters with her camera.

Alonzo says to the crowd, "The moment has arrived

for you to make your presence felt. No longer will you be attacked in silence. The world can now see you taking a courageous stand in a city consumed by fear. What you've experienced has not gone unnoticed. We are not alone any longer and the people of New Orleans can see your faces and understand your suffering. Although you may be forced to leave, we thank you for being here with us today. We understand the risks and we know that you have tried to make a difference for the people of New Orleans."

Ora walks to the center of the steps and says, "As our protest begins, let us remember the pain and humiliation that we have experienced for the last six years in the city. Remember the shame of segregation and the hope taken from us when Huey P. Long was assassinated. We have not been stripped of our dignity. We have become more determined and focused, so that we can stand here today and send a message of peace and faith to the City of New Orleans. We will be remembered for generations to come for our sense of determination. Let us hold up our signs and stand in silent protest until our message has been heard."

Mayor Walmsley walks out to the steps of City Hall with Henry Desmare and Henry Umbach. Walmsley points to Alonzo and says, "Control him," to the policemen. The crowd grows anxious as the police walk over to them and intimidate the protesters.

Ora raises her hands and says, "Remain calm," to the crowd. The horse mounted police encircle the crowd on Saint Charles Avenue and in Lafayette Square. Walmsley is enraged that Alonzo and Ora are able to keep the protesters quiet and calm despite the police presence. The *Times Picayune* photographers capture the horse mounted police as they surround the protesters.

"We should be careful not to have the press cover an attack of the protesters," says Henry Desmare.

"The police will not attack the protesters. The police are here to disburse the crowd. I will do whatever it takes to convince them to give in to the police," says Walmsley.

The protesters stare at Mayor Walmsley knowing that he is angered by their presence. Walmsley is the man they want so desperately to get rid of. They waited for the moment when they would see him during their protest. They wanted to confront him and now he's here to witness their protest in person. They're not intimidated by the police and they would be proud to stand face to face with Mayor Walmsley. As Walmsley walks closer to the crowd, they begin to buzz with anticipation. They stand in disciplined silence to show the press that they are peaceful and nonviolent in every way.

Alonzo turns to Walmsley and stares at the mayor defiantly. He watches as Walmsley orchestrates an intentional disruption of the protest. He knows that the press coverage of the protest is favorable, but he must maintain a careful balance of peace with the crowd. Alonzo is surprised that Walmsley hasn't had him arrested and the protesters attacked. He realizes the impact of the journalists there who have the power to spin the story heavily in favor of the protest. Alonzo knows that his efforts to ensure the presence of the journalists helped to take the protest to the next level. Alonzo begins to imagine the city without Walmsley in office. He thinks about a new mayor who worked closely with Senator Huey P. Long. He looks at Mayor Walmsley and the mess he's made of the city and he's reminded of the purpose of the protest. Alonzo is encouraged at that moment to fight for Walmsley's resignation. He hopes that the press coverage of the protest will generate enough interest in the damage that Walmsley has done in the Black community. The *Times Picayune* journalists begin to photograph Mayor Walmsley as he directs the police to control the protesters. Walmsley is embarrassed by the attention from the press and he begins to leave Henry Desmare and Henry Umbach. "Let's head back inside before they take too many pictures of us out here. I wasn't prepared for this kind of coverage today," says Walmsley.

"Are you going to just leave the protesters out here as they embarrass us?" asks Henry Desmare.

"If I ignore the protesters, they'll give in like they always do," Walmsley says.

"By then, it will be too late," says Henry Desmare.

"Arresting them will create a messy scene for the press. I'll let the police handle the protesters," Walmsley says.

The policeman on guard asks, "Would you like us to get rid of the protesters, Mayor Walmsley?"

"The problem will take care of itself," Walmsley replies sternly. He returns to his office with Henry Desmare and Henry Umbach. Walmsley's office is large and plainly decorated with a bureau and book shelving that covers the white walls.

"Did you have any way of knowing about the protest?" asks Henry Desmare.

"I knew about Alonzo Willis and Ora Lewis, but I never suspected that they would organize a protest here at City Hall," Walmsley replies.

"I would have had the two of them arrested for the crowd to see," says Henry Umbach.

"Arresting the crowd is a last resort at a time like this. The people are suffering a great deal from Huey P. Long's taxing legislation against the city," says Henry Desmare.

"You're right, Henry. The ghost of Long still haunts me. The city is in ruins, because of Long's fight with me," Walmsley says.

"Can you continue to make it through the crash of the city's finances and the protest?" asks Henry Umbach.

"If I begin to lose the support of the people, I'll consider resigning before it gets worse," replies Walmsley surprisingly.

"I'm very disappointed that you would consider resigning," says Henry Desmare.

"I may have no other options," says Walmsley. Henry Desmare and Henry Umbach leave Walmsley's office to give him some time alone.

Ora and Alonzo are relieved to see Walmsley head

back to City Hall. They raise their hands in victory when the door closes behind Walmsley. Many of the people in the crowd clap once Walmsley has left. The horse mounted police leave the crowd and head down Saint Charles Avenue to patrol the street. The remaining police move away from the crowd and monitor them from a distance. Alonzo notices Robert Maestri walk over to City Hall from Lafayette Square. He's glad to see that Robert has made the decision to publicly support the protest. Alonzo's coverage of Robert in the Sepia Socialite had been very favorable and supportive of the young politician.

Alonzo quietly encouraged Robert to take over as mayor if they could force Walmsley to resign. Robert expressed an interest in the mayoral post, but he hesitated to give any public indication of his interest. Robert was a close ally of Huey P. Long. He was appointed to lead the state's Conservation Commission. He knew that there was an immediate need for change, but he wasn't so sure of a solution. When Alonzo invited Robert to the protest he knew the protesters would all be Black, and he assumed that Walmsley would show no mercy. Robert aligned with the Black community the same way that Long embraced them throughout his career. He was not entirely connected to the Black community, but he was kind to Black people.

The idea of a protest at City Hall was radical for Robert, because Walmsley was so volatile. When Robert arrived, he was very surprised to see a crowd of over five hundred Black men and women standing in silent protest. He'd never seen anything quite like it in his life. The protest is very moving to Robert and he immediately realizes the need for him to step in and change the City of New Orleans. Robert lost his sense of determination when Huey P. Long was assassinated and he found it difficult to envision anything too radical in the city. When Alonzo began his coverage of Robert, he was relieved to discover an active vibrant leader in the Black community who wasn't afraid to challenge the establishment. Robert didn't understand how serious Alonzo was about confronting Mayor Walmsley until now. Robert walks over to Alonzo and shakes his hand firmly.

"I'm so glad that you could make it to the protest," says Alonzo.

"Hello, Alonzo. Congratulations for organizing the protest, Ora," Robert says.

"This is a silent protest of Walmsley's abuse. Walmsley sent the police to frighten the crowd on horseback, pushing many of them down," Alonzo explains.

"I'm not surprised at all about Walmsley's antics. I expected the crowd to have been arrested," says Robert.

"The press coverage has been constant. It shielded us from violent treatment by the police. Walmsley actually walked down the steps of City Hall toward the crowd, but he left when he realized that we had not been frightened away by the police," says Alonzo. *Times Picayune* journalists photograph Robert with Alonzo. Robert realizes that he'll be featured in the newspapers with the protesters and he's proud to be there to support their effort. Louise photographs Robert alongside the journalists. Alonzo considers the message that will be sent by the photographs of Robert to the city and their perception of his leadership.

"Please consider sharing a word with the people," Alonzo says to Robert.

"Certainly, Alonzo," says Robert.

Alonzo turns to the crowd and gets their attention. "I'd like to introduce Robert Maestri who is here in support of the protest," says Alonzo as he addresses the crowd. "Robert would like to share a message of hope with you today."

Robert looks out to the crowd and says, "I never

imagined that a fine group of people would gather with such a purpose here at City Hall for the world to see. Not only is the protest peaceful and organized, but it is influential for the challenged leaders of the city. You are all to be commended for your courage. Your presence here today will force us to reject the hate filled traditions of Jim Crow and embrace the freedom that's long overdue for your city." Robert turns to Alonzo and embraces him with a handshake.

"Thank you for your kind words, Robert," says Alonzo. The crowd applauds Robert and buzzes with excitement.

"I'll soon bring an end to the protest, because it has been successful and I don't want Walmsley to begin his attacks again," Alonzo says.

"You're right, Alonzo. We don't want to lose our momentum," says Robert.

"I really couldn't have asked for a better day," Ora says.

"The people have been victorious today. We've done all we can do and should do for the day," Alonzo says.

"I'm finally ready to bring the protest to an end,"

Ora says. Ora walks up to the third step of Gallier Hall. She turns and says to the crowd, "Your presence here today means a great deal to me, to Alonzo Willis and to Robert Maestri. We did not know that today would be such a major success for the people of the City of New Orleans. You have made it a very special day for us. Our work now begins the fight for your freedom. You have given us the strength to press forward despite the hatred and hostility toward our community. You have demonstrated the power of your will and we will represent you relentlessly until our city has been transformed. As we leave City Hall and make our way back to our communities, we will carry these moments in our hearts. Let us never forget this day and the work that we have done in protest." The crowd applauds Ora.

Alonzo walks up the steps to Ora's side. He says, "Our protest has now come to an end. Coverage of the protest will begin and we invite you all to stay active with the Sepia Socialite and our organization." The people begin to return to their cars and walk away from City Hall. The *Times Picayune* journalists and *New Orleans Item* journalists take photographs of Ora, Alonzo and Robert as they shake hands with people in the crowd. Cleo and

Alexia walk over to Ora with Nathan.

"Ma Mere and Ma Mum need to get going, because they're pretty worn out," Nathan says.

"I'm so proud of how well you did today, Ora," says Ellis.

"I knew that you would succeed, Ora," Josephine says. Nathan helps Ellis to his car with Josephine, Cleo and Alexia.

The *Times Picayune* journalists, Carl Johnson and Andrew Fleet approach Alonzo. Carl says, "Hello Alonzo, Ora and Robert. How do you feel about the results of the protest?"

"The protesters were especially calm and serious," replies Alonzo.

"I expected much worse treatment from Walmsley. The fact that no arrests were made is a miracle," Ora says.

"So what do you have in mind next for the people?" asks Carl.

"I will now begin to cover the conditions in the city for Black people as a result of Jim Crow," replies Alonzo.

"Robert, do you have political aspirations?" asks Carl.

"I'm organizing my team to run for a position that

may become open," replies Robert.

"Would you consider running for mayor?" asks Carl.

"I wasn't aware of an opening," replies Robert.

Carl laughs with Andrew and says, "I understand why you would hesitate to declare your interest in the mayor's post."

"I'm very serious about the needs of the city, but I'm unsure of Mayor Walmsley's intentions," says Robert.

"Alonzo and Ora, thank you for allowing us to cover the protest," says Carl.

"The two of you probably saved us all from being arrested and attacked today," says Ora.

"Walmsley came close to having the police attack the protesters, but he didn't want to openly harm them for us to witness his abuse," Carl says.

"You two made all the difference in the world," says Alonzo.

"Remember, we have an event to cover in the French Quarters that's scheduled to begin in an hour," says Andrew.

"Alonzo, we're headed out now. We'll be in touch again soon," Carl says as he leaves with Andrew.

"I expect the coverage of the protest to be thorough," says Alonzo.

"This will be the first time that the press gets the story right on Mayor Walmsley and segregation," Ora says.

"Alonzo, I'd like to meet you at the Sepia Socialite office if I can," Robert says.

"Of course, Robert. I have a lot to discuss with you about politics," Alonzo says. "I'm ready to head back now before Walmsley returns and has a change of heart."

Alonzo, Ora and Louise leave City Hall for Alonzo's car on Girod Street. Ora makes sure that the streets are completely clear and that no signs have been left in the area. She picks up one sign and carries it to the car.

"Ora, you're wise beyond your eighteen years," says Louise. Alonzo, Louise and Ora make it back to Alonzo's car. They climb in and Alonzo turns the ignition on. He drives down Camp Street toward Poydras Street.

"I'm just so relieved that we all survived the protest unharmed by Walmsley," Alonzo says.

"I knew the people could protest peacefully, but I didn't know that Walmsley would refrain from attacking the crowd," says Ora.

"Walmsley is beginning to lose strength," Louise

says. "He's showing signs of concern for his reputation as mayor."

"It won't be too long before Walmsley resigns. When we meet with Robert, I'll asks him to develop a strategy to put pressure on Walmsley and plan his campaign for mayor," Alonzo says. He turns onto Washington Avenue from Broad Avenue.

"Do you think that a campaign may be a bit premature?" Louise asks.

"Robert is ready for a takeover, but he needs our support," Alonzo replies.

"The protest may have convinced Robert of the level of support that he would receive if he actually ran for mayor," says Louise.

"Robert may not be so confident about the support from whites in the city," says Ora.

"That's why the interview and coverage by the *Times Picayune* was so important," Alonzo says.

"When people see Robert in the papers with the protesters, they will be reminded of Huey P. Long," says Louise.

"The protest was so peaceful that people will recognize the importance of the event," says Alonzo.

"People may not identify with the protesters, but at least they'll begin to think about Walmsley's mistreatment of Blacks," says Ora.

"Walmsley has already been heavily criticized by many of the people in the city. He's losing a great deal of support from the Democrats who expected him to recover after the death of Huey P. Long," Alonzo says.

"Long's political machine overwhelmed Walmsley and the Old Regulars haven't seen him return to his original form," says Louise.

"Walmsley lost credibility during Long's administration," Ora says.

"Without the support of the Old Regulars, Walmsley has very little leverage and power. He's a shadow of his previous self," says Alonzo. He arrives at the office and he sees Robert Maestri sitting in his car outside. Alonzo parks in the driveway and lets Louise and Ora out of the car. The neighbors clap and cheer for Alonzo and Ora. They all wave at the neighbors and smile. Alonzo walks over to greet Robert and says, "Come on inside. We have a lot to talk about with you." Louise opens the front door for Alonzo and Robert. Robert follows Alonzo into the office and they have a seat at his desk.

"So how did the day begin?" asks Robert.

"Most of the protesters were here waiting at the office for us to arrive this morning. They were organized and focused," replies Alonzo.

"The protesters seemed to be very clear about their objective. Their spirits overwhelmed Walmsley," Robert says.

"Walmsley might have experienced a moment of grace when he realized that the protesters were so peaceful," Ora says.

"Walmsley may have experienced grace, but his mercy was self-serving," Robert says.

"Robert, what would it take for you to announce your intentions to run for mayor?" Alonzo asks.

"I am patiently waiting for Walmsley to resign," replies Robert.

"I'd like to continue my coverage of you and begin to highlight your qualifications for a political position," Alonzo says.

"I'm in favor of the coverage, but I'm concerned that Walmsley might overreact to any indication that I might be interested in running for mayor," Robert says.

"Remember that the *Times Picayune* coverage will

discuss your interest in the mayoral position," says Alonzo.

"You're right about the *Times Picayune* coverage, but I'd like to wait until their articles have been released and Walmsley has reacted to the interview," insists Robert.

"You're right. Let's be patient," Alonzo says. "Do you feel more confident about the support for a Walmsley resignation now that you've experienced the protest?"

"I definitely feel better now that I've seen so many people put everything on the line to confront Walmsley. I'd like to see significant support from whites in the city for a Walmsley resignation," says Robert.

"Many of them have voiced their concerns about Walmsley, but the press has not actively published articles on the disappointments of the people," Alonzo says.

"The real test will be Walmsley's response in the press to the coverage of the protest," says Robert.

"Walmsley will try everything that he can to discredit the protesters. He'll pressure the people to change their perception of the protesters and demonize their message," says Alonzo.

"Walmsley's story twisting antics won't work this time. His days are numbered," Robert says.

"Robert, thank you for stopping by to meet with

us," Alonzo says as he shakes his hand.

"I'm glad to have been invited," Robert says.

"I know that you will be mayor someday," Ora says.

Robert laughs and says, "You might be right, but Walmsley won't go down without a fight." Alonzo walks Robert to the front door. The bells chime overhead.

"I look forward to seeing you again soon," Alonzo says. Robert waves goodbye to Alonzo and climbs into his car. He drives away. Alonzo closes the door behind him.

"Robert has a lot of potential, but he's afraid of taking risks," Alonzo says.

"You should run for Mayor if Robert is afraid," suggests Ora. Louise and Alonzo laugh with Ora.

"Do you have enough material to cover the protest in time for Friday's issue, Louise?" asks Alonzo.

"I have more photographs than the *Times Picayune* and the *New Orleans Item* journalists, because I began early this morning during the gathering here at the office," replies Louise.

"I'm eager to write about the success of the protest," Ora says.

"We have a lot of work to do throughout the week, but the larger newspapers will give us a big boost," Alonzo

says.

"It will be wonderful to finally be featured in a positive light by the *Times Picayune* after working so hard to build interest in Walmsley's segregation abuses," Louise says.

"There's always some chance that Walmsley will influence the press and ruin our hopes of reaching the city," Ora says.

"You're right, Ora but I doubt that Walmsley could destroy our efforts this time," says Alonzo. "You should get home to celebrate the day's victory with your grandmothers and father."

"I'm really looking forward to celebrating with them," says Ora. Alonzo and Louise walk Ora out to their car in the driveway. Alonzo opens the car door for Ora and Louise and they climb into the car.

"I was so glad to see the expressions on Josephine's and Ellis' faces at City Hall," Louise says.

"They were very vocal during the planning stages of the protest," says Ora.

"Josephine and Ellis probably inspired you to organize the protest just by being so supportive of you," Alonzo says.

"If it weren't for Josephine, you could not have become a member of the writing staff, Ora," says Louise.

"You're right, Louise. I really appreciate all that Josephine and Ellis have helped you to do, Ora," Alonzo says. He turns onto Broad Avenue toward Tulane Avenue. He thinks about the day that Walmsley had them stopped by the police after meeting with Huey P. Long. He considers the possibility of his arrest today.

"It's not going to happen again. Don't worry, Alonzo. Walmsley is not coming after you this time," says Louise.

"I hope you're right, Louise. I'm ready for just about anything with Walmsley now that we've held the protest," Alonzo says.

"Walmsley has a much bigger problem to handle now with the press and the Old Regulars. He won't try any of his old games with us anymore," Louise says.

Alonzo turns onto Claiborne Avenue from Tulane Avenue. He notices a police car up ahead, but it turns before it approaches his car. Alonzo is relieved, but he knows that Walmsley is waiting for his chance to retaliate against them all. When he saw Walmsley at City Hall today he really didn't know what to expect. Now that the protest is in the history books, Alonzo is nervously anticipating a quiet attack from Walmsley that may be more dangerous than anything he's done in the past. Alonzo realizes that he has very few powerful allies capable of dealing with Walmsley.

"Walmsley may strike at any time. I understood the risks when I began to plan the protest," Ora says.

"Walmsley always has the last word on segregation. He's dangerous, but we shouldn't try to anticipate his next move," says Louise.

"Walmsley will definitely lash out at us, but he's so different now that Huey P. Long is gone," says Ora.

"I have no regrets. I wouldn't change anything about the day at all," says Alonzo. He arrives at Ora's home on Annette Street.

Louise climbs out of the car and reaches over to give Ora a hug. "You were outstanding today, Ora," says Louise.

"Thank you, Louise. I'll see you tomorrow, Alonzo," Ora says as she waves goodbye. Alonzo waves goodbye to Ora and drives away with Louise. Ora enters the house and everyone's inside waiting for her to arrive.

Nathan embraces Ora. "I knew that you could

successfully lead the protest, Ora," he says.

Josephine walks over to hug Ora. "You did so well at City Hall," she says.

"Ora, you're a genius, honey," says Ellis.

"How was your meeting with Alonzo and Louise at the office after the protest?" Nathan asks.

"Robert Maestri met with us at the office. Alonzo is trying to convince Robert to contest Walmsley outright," Ora replies.

"It may take some time before Robert is ready to fight Walmsley openly. I'm just so relieved that there were no arrests at City Hall today," says Nathan.

"Alonzo was almost certain that Walmsley would have us arrested. He was overjoyed by the results of the day," Ora says.

"I would have liked to have met with Robert," Nathan says.

"Alonzo has more strength than Robert right now. Robert has a lot of thinking to do," Ora says.

"Can you believe the press coverage that the protest received?" asks Josephine.

"Alonzo did an excellent job of planning the coverage for the protest," Nathan says.

"I had no idea that the protest would be such a major success," Cleo says.

"I knew that Alonzo was capable of pulling off a peaceful protest that would influence the city in a powerful way. Despite all of my hesitations about Walmsley, I was convinced that Alonzo was prepared and focused enough to protect us and organize us," Nathan says.

"Once you committed to take part in the protest, I was convinced that we would succeed," Ora says.

"I would have been so disappointed if I'd missed the day with you," Nathan says. "You've done something that was nearly impossible for the city."

"Did you ever imagine that your eighteen-year-old daughter would accomplish so much?" asks Josephine.

Nathan laughs and replies, "Ora is a very special girl. She has the faith of her mother and me combined."

"What if you'd forbidden Ora from leading the protest?" asks Cleo.

"I would have made a big mistake to discourage Ora from leading the people. She deserves this moment after working so hard to fight desegregation and losing Huey P. Long," Nathan replies.

"Nathan, please join us for lunch," Ellis says.

"I'd be glad to share lunch with you," Nathan says. Josephine sets the dining room table for the meal. Ellis finishes her preparation of steamed rainbow trout, sautéed carrots and rice pilaf.

"Would you like help in the kitchen, Ma Mum?" offers Ora.

"No, Ora. You should rest and enjoy the meal," Ellis says. Nathan, Cleo and Ora have a seat at the table. Alexia helps Ellis and Josephine serve the food.

Nathan prays saying, "God thank you for your mercy and kindness. Thank you for your grace. Thank you for an uplifting day. Bless this meal and our families, so that we may worship your holy name. Amen." Ellis and Josephine have a seat at the dining room table. "This food is delicious, Ma Mum," Nathan says.

"Thank you, Nathan. I'm so glad you could join us," says Ellis.

"Papa, I still can't believe that you approved of the protest," says Alexia.

"I always expected Papa to object to Ora's confrontation with Walmsley and other racists," Cleo says.

"Papa's approval and support means so much to me," Ora says.

"The time has come for you to determine your own destiny, Ora. I was ready to help you face the consequences of a fight with Walmsley no matter how severe they might be," Nathan says.

"You inspired me to lead the protest despite your many warnings, Papa. I owe my success to you," says Ora.

"Remember the continuous encouragement from Ma Mere and Ma Mum," Nathan says.

"Ma Mum and Ma Mere have given my life a sense of purpose from the beginning. Without them, I could never have become a journalist or lead a protest," Ora says.

"Ora, you're so much like your mother, because you never quit," says Ellis.

"Ora, you have a gift of faith that is so special to me," says Josephine.

"You can change the city, Ora. You have my full support from now on," Alexia says.

"I still feel like the same girl who would beg Alonzo to publish my letters on Walmsley. To think that everyone now believes in me is pure grace," Ora says.

"You convinced me when Alonzo called me with details on the plans for the protest. Alonzo was so serious and so determined to succeed that I could not deny you the chance to fight segregation peacefully," Nathan says.

"You've really changed my assumptions about your concerns, Papa," Ora says.

"My concerns still exist, but I trust Alonzo's judgment a great deal more now," Nathan says. Alexia begins to clear the table for her grandmothers.

"Would you like some praline candy?" offers Ellis.

"I'd enjoy a praline. It's been so long since I had some," Nathan replies. Alexia brings the tray of pralines to her father.

"Are you ready for Ora to really succeed when Walmsley resigns?" asks Josephine.

"I'm definitely ready for Ora's victory. Walmsley will resign once the press coverage of the protest begins to take effect," Nathan says.

"The press coverage will bury Walmsley in criticism. He'll never be able to recover," Ora says.

"You've backed Walmsley into a tight corner with no defense," says Cleo.

"Walmsley should have resigned months ago when Huey P. Long exposed him for plotting his assassination," Alexia says.

"Walmsley will not resign until he completely loses

support from the Old Regulars political machine," Ora says. "The protest was the most effective way to expose Walmsley's abuse of Black people and the damage done by segregation."

"The Old Regulars will not tolerate the embarrassment in the press and Walmsley's loss of control of the city. They will certainly demand his resignation," Nathan says.

"Alonzo will work with the press to provide them with details on the many attacks by Walmsley's men throughout the city," says Ora.

"I'm here to support your work and I'm confident that Alonzo will get it done," says Nathan.

"I love you very much, Papa. I couldn't have imagined a better day to spend with you," says Ora.

"This is what I imagined for you for years and now you're at the center of it all in the fight against segregation," Nathan says.

"I know you must leave for Baton Rouge, but I'm going to miss you so much, Papa," says Ora.

"I'll be back soon to show my support. Call me each day to let me know about any dangers you face," Nathan says.

"I will call you daily," says Ora. Nathan stands up from the table and enters the living room. Alexia gives Nathan a hug. Cleo shakes his father's hand. Ora hugs Nathan and says, "It means so much to me for you to be a part of my efforts."

"Goodbye, Nathan," Josephine says.

"I look forward to seeing you again soon, Nathan," says Ellis. Ora walks her father to his car outside.

"Stay strong and don't give up," Nathan says.

"I won't give up. We will soon have a new mayor. Believe me. Victory will be ours," Ora declares.

CHAPTER 8 / "WALMSLEY'S LAST WORDS"

Ora jumps out of bed and runs down the hallway to the bathroom. She hops in the shower and runs water on her sleepy face. When she finishes her shower she quickly dries off and brushes her teeth. Ora throws on her robe and rushes back to her room to change her clothes. Josephine has prepared Ora's outfit for her morning meeting with Mayor Walmsley. She changes into the royal blue shift styled dress, lace slip and matching blue flats. Ora walks out to the kitchen and greets her grandmothers. "Good morning, Ma Mere and Ma Mum," she says.

"Hi there, Ora. Are you ready?" asks Josephine.

"I still can't believe Walmsley requested the meeting at all," replies Ora. "I'm not really sure what to expect."

"Walmsley will probably ask you, Nathan and Alonzo to bring an end to your coverage against his attacks," Josephine says.

"Walmsley asked Alonzo to meet with him about the protest," Ora says.

"Walmsley is playing games with you and Alonzo. He's trying to intimidate you face to face," Josephine says.

"Walmsley is quite capable of having us arrested today at City Hall to finally get rid of us," Ora says.

"If Walmsley wanted to arrest you, he would have done it a long time ago," reasons Josephine.

"Ora, breakfast has been prepared for you. Are you hungry or too nervous about your day?" asks Ellis.

"Thank you, Ma Mum. I am very nervous, but I'm hungry enough to eat," replies Ora.

Ellis hands Ora a plate of toast, grits, bacon and scrambled eggs. "Here you are, Ora. Try to eat as much as you can," she says.

Ora's father knocks at the front door. Josephine

walks over to answer the door. "Good morning, Nathan. You're early today," she says.

Nathan enters the house. "You never can be too early for Walmsley. He's a real piece of work," he says.

"Come on in. Ora is having breakfast. Have you already eaten?" asks Josephine.

"Yes, I have. I can sit with her while she eats," replies Nathan. He enters the kitchen and takes a seat next to Ora at the table.

"Good morning, Papa. How are you?" asks Ora.

"I'm not very happy this morning, Ora. I won't be happy until Walmsley finally resigns. Today's meeting is a reminder of Walmsley's continuous hold on the city. He refuses to give in and now he wants to convince us to stop our coverage of his abuse. He's unbelievable," replies Nathan.

"Walmsley has never been so vulnerable. He's hoping for a truce of mercy from us, but he knows that we would have to be coerced," Ora says.

"Ora, you know how I feel about you making contact with Walmsley. I'm not surprised that he asked me to be there as well," Nathan says.

"Nathan, you've made a strong impression on

Walmsley. He can't ignore what you've done with Alonzo and Ora. He's compelled to change your impression of him," says Josephine.

"Nothing can change my impression of Walmsley. He's a violent racist leader who's lost touch with the people," Nathan says.

"Papa, I'm just so glad that you decided to join us and that you're allowing me to meet with him. This is not exactly what I had in mind, but it's good that Walmsley is acknowledging our influence," Ora says.

"After the protest, you worked very hard to cover Walmsley and his segregationist attacks. There have been many risks involved, but you exposed his abuses," says Nathan.

"I often considered what it would be like to meet Walmsley in person, but I honestly wasn't prepared for a meeting," says Ora.

"You can do it, Ora. We're praying for you. You're going to be just fine today," assures Josephine.

Ora finishes her breakfast and clears the table. "Thank you for breakfast, Ma Mum," she says.

"You're welcome, Ora. I have to keep you strong," Ellis says.

"It's time to head over to Alonzo's office to meet with them before the Walmsley appointment," Nathan says.

"You two be careful at City Hall," says Ellis.

"We'll be back before you know it," says Ora. Nathan and Ora walk through the living room to the front door. Nathan opens the door for Ora.

"Just remember that we're here for you no matter what happens," says Josephine.

"I won't ever forget, Ma Mere," Ora says. Nathan and Ora walk down to his car. Nathan opens the door for Ora and she climbs into the car. Nathan walks around to the driver's side and enters. Josephine waves goodbye. Nathan drives down Annette Street toward Claiborne Avenue.

"Ora, I'm beginning to lose my patience with Walmsley. This is the last time that I'll make contact with him before he resigns," Nathan says.

"Papa, I understand. We all want Walmsley to just give in, but he won't let go. The Old Regulars have even asked for his resignation," says Ora.

"If the Old Regulars can't convince him to quit, how can we stop him?" asks Nathan.

"Walmsley knows that we have organized the people against him. That's the only reason he's asked us to meet with him," Ora replies.

"Perhaps we should have declined the meeting and continued our criticism of his Jim Crow attacks," Nathan says.

"If we declined, we wouldn't have had an opportunity to finally confront Walmsley without the crowds and the distractions," says Ora.

"I just don't feel comfortable about being alone with Walmsley in a room. He's a very dangerous man," says Nathan.

"Papa, I assure you that Walmsley won't harm us in any way today," Ora says.

"Ora, what if you're wrong? What if he's waiting there at City Hall right now to have us arrested?" asks Nathan. He turns onto Washington Avenue toward Erato Street.

"I'll take full responsibility for everything Walmsley does to us today," replies Ora.

"You cannot turn it around once it's done, Ora. We're at the mercy of Walmsley today," Nathan says.

"Aren't we always at the mercy of Walmsley, Papa?" asks Ora.

"Ora, you're right. All we can do is confront him

and surround him with coverage that exposes his attacks," says Nathan. He pulls up to Alonzo's office and parks the car. Ora climbs out of the car and follows her father to the front door of the office.

Louise opens the door for Nathan. The bells chime overhead. "Good morning, Nathan and Ora. We're glad you're here early," she says.

Alonzo approaches Nathan and shakes his hand. "Nathan, having you here is very encouraging for me. Sometimes I just don't know how to handle Mayor Walmsley," he says.

"Everything you've done has prepared you for this day. Whether Walmsley listens to us or he chooses to attack us, remember that you've given your all to bringing an end to segregation in the city," says Nathan.

"We've been fighting with Walmsley for months and he doesn't seem to let up. We had no idea that he wanted to actually meet with us," Louise says.

"The meeting is a pretext for the compromise that Walmsley wants from us. He can force us to compromise or he can persuade us carefully. He's a snake and he knows it," Nathan says.

"Let's work on what we'd like to say to Walmsley

today if he gives us a chance," Alonzo says.

"We'd like to discuss the arrests and attacks on Blacks in the city. We'd like Walmsley to know about the attacks, so that he can acknowledge them and devise a plan to bring them to an end if he's not actually responsible," Louise says.

"If Walmsley can address segregation in the city and the firing of Blacks from municipal positions, we'd make some progress," says Ora.

"Ora, the only progress that can be made is to force Walmsley to resign. He'll never be a righteous mayor," Nathan says.

"New Orleans is such a special city. Our culture is so rich and our people are unique. We deserve to have a mayor who's just," Louise says.

"I accepted this meeting with Walmsley to confront him and ask him to stop his abuse of Black people. My expectations were never really high," Alonzo says.

"If Walmsley could eliminate us, he would. He just wants to control us and stop the press coverage of his attacks," Nathan says.

"Nathan, what would you like to say to Walmsley today?" asks Alonzo.

"I really don't have anything to say to Walmsley. I just want him to know that I'm here to protect my daughter and I don't want anything to happen to her," Nathan replies.

"That's all we can ask you to do, Nathan. We understand your concerns and we're here for you," Alonzo says.

"We should get ready to leave for City Hall soon," Louise says.

"Ora, are you ready to finally meet Walmsley in person?" asks Alonzo.

"I'm not so sure. I'm afraid of him right now. I stood up to him once, but the circumstances were different. I'm not sure of how to address him today," Ora says.

"Ora, we understand. You're just eighteen years old. There's no way for you to be prepared for a circumstance like this. Just listen carefully and try not to be intimidated by Walmsley," Alonzo says.

"Ora doesn't really have to be there. She can stay here while we meet with Walmsley," Nathan says.

"Walmsley's expecting Ora today. He asked me about her specifically," Alonzo says.

"Something just doesn't feel right about this meeting. Walmsley's racism concerns me," Nathan says.

"If we don't like what he says, we can leave," Alonzo says.

"I doubt that he'll let us walk out on our meeting if we disagree," Nathan says.

"Let's think about what we'll say and do during the meeting," suggests Louise.

"We can enter Walmsley's office and listen to what he has to say. If he allows us to speak, we can describe the abuse that Blacks have endured during his administration," Alonzo says.

"If the meeting becomes too intense, we can ask him to wrap it up," Nathan says.

"It might not be so easy. He probably won't let us leave until we agree to stop the coverage of his attacks," Louise says.

"Maybe I should stay here and skip the meeting," Ora says.

"No, Ora. We need you there with us today," says Alonzo.

"Ora, it's alright. Come with us and have the experience of meeting Walmsley face to face after trying so hard," Nathan says.

"You'll regret it if you stay behind. Try not to worry

so much, Ora," says Louise.

"If Walmsley talks about the protest, let's change the subject to his attacks. We don't want him to back us against a wall about the effort," says Alonzo.

"I'd be surprised if he mentions Huey P. Long at all, but I wouldn't put it past him. Let's avoid the topic if we can," Nathan says.

"I'm just so nervous about Walmsley's aggression. No matter how hard we try, he'll pressure us into silence and submission with threats," says Ora.

"I'll handle the threats. Just stay focused on desegregation," Alonzo says.

"Well, I'm ready to get to City Hall now. I don't want to linger and let Walmsley get to me today," Nathan says.

"Alright, let's get going," Alonzo says as he leads Louise, Ora and Nathan to the front door. The bells chime overhead as he opens the door. They walk out to the driveway and Alonzo opens the car doors. Ora and Nathan climb into the back seats. Alonzo backs out onto Erato Street toward Washington Avenue. "I have a good feeling about today's meeting," he says.

"What's on your mind?" Nathan asks.

"Walmsley will resign very soon," Alonzo replies.

"That would be perfect," says Ora.

"We have to keep working on it. We can't let up," Alonzo says.

"This meeting is a sign of Walmsley's weakness. He never would have requested a meeting while Huey P. Long was alive," Louise says.

"The protest really took a toll on Walmsley. He said that it was the reason he requested the meeting," Alonzo says.

"Why would Walmsley wait so long after the protest to request a meeting with us?" asks Nathan.

"He didn't realize how damaging the press coverage of the protest would be until now. He hasn't been able to regain control of the press since then," replies Alonzo.

"Press coverage means a lot to Walmsley. He shows an entirely different face to the press than the one we know. That's what has always made him so dangerous," Ora says.

"Ora, this meeting and everything we've done recently is a direct result of your efforts and disappointment with Walmsley. The meeting just wouldn't be the same without you," Alonzo says.

"I wanted to see Walmsley resign before we would

ever have to actually meet with him. I feel like I've failed in some way," Ora says.

"You haven't failed. You've succeeded. This meeting is just a formality before the resignation," says Nathan.

"Your father is right. Be patient with yourself and with us. It's just a matter of time before Walmsley resigns," Alonzo says. He turns onto Poydras Street from Broad Avenue. His heartbeat quickens and the blood rushes through his veins as he draws closer to City Hall. Alonzo knows that the meeting with Walmsley will be intense, but he's not quite prepared for the confrontation. He's physically upset by Walmsley, although his mind is focused. Alonzo always avoided Walmsley and closely followed Huey P. Long. His approach to Walmsley was a proactive connection to Long, reporting all of the attacks and abuse to the Senator. He never imagined that he would be left to defend himself against Walmsley. When Long was assassinated, Alonzo avoided Walmsley until his attacks became too violent. Alonzo found the strength to support Ora's protest and expose Walmsley's abuse of the Black community. Alonzo was finally able to shift the momentum of the press in their favor, despite Walmsley's constant pressure.

When Walmsley's office contacted Alonzo to request the meeting, he was very surprised. He never thought that Walmsley would contact him directly. The call was brief and stern. Walmsley's secretary, Karen Margeaux was polite, but she was obviously upset with Alonzo on the phone. Karen asked Alonzo to have Nathan and Ora join him at the meeting with Walmsley. Alonzo asked Karen why the invitation was made and she said that Walmsley needed to speak with him about the protest. Alonzo quickly ended the call and agreed to meet with Walmsley.

When Alonzo explained to Nathan that Walmsley requested the meeting, he was angry. Nathan had no intention of listening to Walmsley cloak his violence. Alonzo convinced Nathan to join him, but it was very difficult to do. Alonzo didn't want to have to explain to Walmsley that Nathan and Ora wouldn't be able to attend the meeting. He was relieved when Nathan finally gave in to Walmsley's request. Ora was initially excited that Walmsley would invite them to City Hall, but her excitement soon waned. She quickly realized that Walmsley's intentions were less than noble. When Nathan called her about Walmsley, he warned her that the meeting was just another plot to regain control of the press. Ora lost hope for a conciliatory meeting of the minds, and prepared herself for the worst. She didn't consider the possibility of reconciliation from Walmsley any longer after discussing the invitation with her father. She settled for simply making it through the day unscathed.

Alonzo sincerely hoped for brighter days, but he recognized Ora's youth and inexperience with white supremacists. He'd always thought of Ora as idealistic and innocent. He did eventually begin to appreciate her courage and genius, but it didn't come easy for Alonzo. Ora possesses the great qualities of her very dignified father who'd served Great Britain during the First World War, but she also has a certain level of vulnerability that comes from losing her mother at the age of seven. To Alonzo, Ora is a complex reflection of her very talented and dedicated family, and he feels obligated to help her reach her full potential. He's not naive about her passionate stance against segregation and he works constantly to protect her from racist aggressors. He's just proud to finally be able to translate Ora's gifts into success for the Sepia Socialite and a means for her sustenance.

When Alonzo and Louise finally made the decision

to hire Ora full-time as a staff writer, they were ecstatic. To know that Ora's grandmothers would have the help that they needed and that Ora would be able to write professionally was a blessing. The results were undeniable. When they allowed Ora to cover the shooting at City Hall, they'd never sold more copies of their newspaper since its establishment. Ora had an immediate impact on sales. She has a golden touch and Alonzo knows it. Without Ora, the paper would be average.

Alonzo's only concern is that Ora would sacrifice her studies. High school is a privilege for young Black women, and Alonzo doesn't want her to suffer the consequences. Yet, he realizes that Ora's talent is undeniable. His first impression of Ora was that she was stubborn and detached. He soon realizes that Ora's persistence is invaluable. Alonzo assumed that Ora's writing would alienate her from her peers, but she was socially gifted in an unusually powerful way. Not only had Ora turned out to be an exceptional desegregation writer, but it was apparent that she was a wonderful person.

Alonzo discovered that he could depend upon Ora for just about anything involving the paper. She worked long nights and she wrote the articles that no one dared to write about pain and suffering in the roughest areas of the city. Many people called Alonzo's office asking for Ora to cover their stories. Ora had an immediate impact on the Sepia Socialite and its community of readers. Alonzo was so surprised by Huey P. Long's reaction to Ora. She seemingly transformed into a real journalist in a matter of days. Had Alonzo completely missed Ora's talents when he denied publication of her many letters? He often wonders if Ora is God appointed in his life. Her maturity and focus affirm her rightful place on his small staff.

When Ora writes, people listen. Alonzo learns not to trust his instincts with Ora and to trust her sincerity. Today's meeting with Walmsley could be a turning point for Alonzo and the entire community, but he knows that he's facing a nearly impossible challenge. Alonzo's dream is that the city would be restored. Walmsley stands firmly in the way of this vision.

Alonzo hopes that Huey P. Long's vision for the City of New Orleans can be made real. He works so hard to make this possible for the Black community and for everyone. Yet, Alonzo is overwhelmed by hatred from Walmsley and the many white supremacists in the state. As Alonzo drives to City Hall, he is reminded of the extreme acts of violence in Louisiana against Black people that hardly compares to Walmsley's attacks. Despite his anxiety, Alonzo is ready to face Walmsley and give him a piece of his mind. He's ready to show Ora a better way to deal with white supremacists. Alonzo parks his car on Camp Street two blocks away from City Hall. He opens the doors for Louise and Ora. Nathan climbs out of the car and follows Alonzo to Saint Charles Avenue.

"The moment has arrived. Are we all ready?" asks Louise.

"I'm ready to get in there and get out of there as quickly as we can," says Nathan.

"If we can survive the first ten minutes, we can make it through the entire meeting," Alonzo says.

"I won't say a word unless Walmsley directly addresses me," Ora says. She grabs her father's hand. Nathan shakes her arm and tugs her closer to him. "Ora, this is all your fault, you know. The protest changed everything for Walmsley. I'm placing the blame on you for this one," Nathan says.

"Papa, if I didn't organize the protest and cover Walmsley, what would you have done about it?" asks Ora.

"Just calm down and let's head inside. We'll find out

today if you were right after all," Nathan says. They climb the stairs of City Hall.

Ora thinks back to the day of the protest. She remembers the expression on Walmsley's face when he walked out to see the crowd. Ora thinks about the protesters and their hope for desegregation. The meeting with Walmsley is an unexpected result from an effort intended to eliminate the mayor from city government altogether. As Ora walks toward the City Hall entrance, she is reminded of the many people in her community who have been hurt by Mayor Walmsley. She searches for strength to face him and change his oppressive mind. Ora is afraid, but she's not overwhelmed by the intensity of the moment. She's fought so hard to stop Walmsley, and she's prepared to continue until her work is done.

Nathan opens the door for Ora and says, "Let's head inside, Ora. We don't want the mayor to wait too long."

"We have a little time before the meeting, but it's always better to be early," says Alonzo. Nathan follows Alonzo down the hall to the mayor's office. Alonzo opens the door for Louise and Ora. He sees Mayor Walmsley's secretary, Karen Margeaux and says, "Good morning. I am Alonzo Willis. We are here to meet with the mayor."

"Mayor Walmsley will be available soon. His morning briefing will conclude in a moment. Please stand here and do not touch anything in the office," says Karen. Nathan stands next to Ora. Alonzo and Louise stand together near Ora. Mayor Walmsley calls Karen on the phone and asks her to bring Alonzo and the group into his office.

Karen walks over to Alonzo and says, "Mayor Walmsley is ready to see you now. Please follow me." Alonzo follows Karen into Walmsley's office. "Mayor Walmsley, this is Alonzo Willis, Ora Lewis, Nathan Lewis and Louise Willis," she says.

"Please come in. There's no need to sit, because this meeting will be brief, Alonzo. Karen, that will be all," Walmsley commands. Karen leaves the room and closes the doors behind her. Alonzo stands near Mayor Walmsley. Nathan stands beside Alonzo. Louise and Ora stand together behind Alonzo and Nathan. "I was told that you know why I invited you here today, Alonzo," Walmsley says.

"Yes, Karen explained that you wanted to meet with us about the City Hall protest," replies Alonzo.

Walmsley begins to scream. "Alonzo, not only am I

angry about the protest, but your coverage has been too critical!" Walmsley exclaims. Alonzo is shocked that Walmsley would yell. He stares at the mayor despondently and doesn't respond. Nathan and Ora look over at each in disappointment. "Alonzo, I will not tolerate your disrespect. Answer me, boy!" yells Walmsley.

"Mayor Walmsley, we agreed to meet with you today to discuss the conditions of the city. We are not here to be berated," says Alonzo.

"I've never heard of something so ridiculous. Do you really believe the garbage that you print on me? Do you know who I really am?" asks Walmsley.

"The people know who you really are and they're devastated by the violence in the city," replies Alonzo.

"I have nothing to do with the attacks that you claim are made by me or my staff. Stop printing false claims in your paper!" Walmsley shouts as he raises his hands in frustration.

"Every attack that we cover is accurate and genuine. We have evidence of a direct connection to your administration, Mayor Walmsley," Alonzo explains.

"Alonzo, I may ask you to leave. You're not being honest, and you don't understand the damage that you've done to my administration!" shouts Walmsley.

"Mayor Walmsley, I apologize for all errors made in reporting on our part. It is never our intention to print stories that aren't true. You deserve honesty, and so do we," Alonzo says.

"You will never mention my name again in your newspaper, Alonzo Willis!" Walmsley demands. Alonzo nods his head in compliance and looks over to Nathan for a reaction. Nathan is visibly distraught about Walmsley's shouting and commands. He stares at Walmsley in disgust. "Do not contact other members of the press in New Orleans, Baton Rouge or anywhere else about me as your mayor. Do I make myself clear?" asks Walmsley.

"We do understand, Mayor Walmsley. Consider it done," replies Alonzo. Walmsley calms down considerably. He scans the room for defiance, and he's satisfied with the reactions of the group. Walmsley is a survivor of tough politics in a city dominated by the Mafia. He's a conservative leader in an unconventional diverse city with multicultural traditions. He fought hard to claim victory in an election heavily influenced by Huey P. Long. He was nearly impossible to beat, but Walmsley somehow prevailed. Walmsley would do anything and everything to

finally rid himself of Huey P. Long, and his desperation
was ultimately revealed by Long himself. Walmsley never
recovered from the assassination plot scandal, especially
after Long was actually murdered by Dr. Carl Weiss. Many
of Walmsley's original supporters began to distance
themselves from him as the city sank into a murky
quagmire of financial decay.

With Senator Long gone, Walmsley is finally able
to unleash a pogrom of terror on the Black community. He
has them killed, shot, beaten and arrested under the guise of
the White League supremacists. There is very little
evidence that connects Walmsley to the attacks, but
everyone knows of his involvement. He demands silence
from Alonzo, Ora and Nathan, because he knows that
they're the driving force behind the movement that
threatens his authority. Without them, the Black
community would be in disarray as they search for a
solution to his deadly agenda. Walmsley knows that
Alonzo will not simply disappear, but his dire warning will
slow him down enough to give the mayor some time to
recover. Walmsley has never had Alonzo or Ora arrested,
because he refuses to make martyrs of them. However, the
possibility is tempting to him.

The Old Regulars approached Walmsley about a resignation soon after the protest, and he seriously began to consider leaving city government. Yet, Walmsley was certain that he could control the protesters and all of his opponents to regain power in the city. He was very surprised to see a woman like Ora lead an actual protest. Walmsley assumed that Alonzo was relatively quiet and focused on the success of his newspaper. He didn't know that Alonzo and Ora would take it so far.

Alonzo rarely questioned Walmsley's authority in his paper before Long's assassination. Alonzo was fairly predictable as a journalist and leader. Walmsley assumed that Alonzo feared him and he never suspected that he would be so rebellious. Walmsley knew that Alonzo was very well connected, but he didn't understand that he was capable of a complete transformation of segregation press coverage. Walmsley had a stronghold on the press in New Orleans and the surrounding regions throughout his administration. No Black leaders had ever challenged his dominance of the press until Alonzo organized the protest.

Walmsley felt betrayed by the press after the protest. The journalists who would normally depict him as an intelligent, capable leader, relinquished their captive audience and silently watched as the tides were turned. Walmsley believed that he was lenient and patient with the protesters and he didn't understand how the press could be so critical of his reaction to the effort. He never made the connection of the protest to his many attacks.

Having Alonzo and Ora in his office is actually very positive for Walmsley, because they're seemingly attentive and remorseful. Walmsley can see the expressions on their faces and he perceives sorrow from Alonzo. Although Walmsley is angry, he's not entirely enraged with the four of them. Walmsley honestly hopes to be able to resign in peace with a conservative successor in place, but he knows that it's nearly impossible in light of the negative press coverage. If he resigns, he'll give in to the Long political machine. They will take over the city and trample over his white supremacist agenda. Walmsley resisted Long in every possible way, but he cannot defeat him, even in death.

Walmsley represented the privileged white upper class in a city divided by race. He held on to Jim Crow traditions like a gospel. He preached a message of hatred that resonated with whites engaged in class struggle that they simply couldn't win during the Great Depression.

Walmsley lost the fight for economic reforms of the city finances and drove New Orleans further into its own devastating depression. He didn't understand why state legislators opposed him so strongly as mayor. The Old Regulars were beginning to lose patience with Walmsley's diplomatic failures. Not only had the state legislature stripped him of all fiscal powers, but people were in an uproar about his mistreatment of Blacks. To regain power as a political organization, the Old Regulars sought to eliminate Walmsley and essentially appoint his replacement. There was very little that Walmsley could do to repair the fragmented relations with the organization that supported his first campaign for mayor. Walmsley fights so many factions, but he cannot stop the Old Regulars. They have the power to make or break politicians, and they have their sights set on replacing him.

Walmsley doesn't have the strength to fight the Old Regulars. He's only able to throw his weight around in poor vulnerable areas like the Black community. He knows that he'd never be able to silence white members of the press. Walmsley even considers having Alonzo print something positive on him, but he'd rather cut him off altogether. "The City of New Orleans is in ruins, Alonzo. We need all the positive press coverage that we can get. Your stories are divisive and they add fuel to the fire for the already hostile state legislature. Don't you understand what you've done? You've destroyed my credibility in the state," says Walmsley.

"Mayor Walmsley, please excuse me, but aren't you aware of the murders, shootings and attacks of Black people in the city?" asks Nathan.

"Nathan, the City of New Orleans is a very violent place. There's a lot of crime here. Black and white people die all the time. You should know that I'm tough on crime. This is my city and I do everything in my power to keep it safe," replies Walmsley.

"Mayor, what Nathan means is, are you aware of white supremacist violence in the city?" asks Alonzo.

"Nathan and Alonzo, I am a white supremacist. I do not believe that whites and Blacks are equal. When I see fighting or I hear of violence against Blacks, I choose not to get involved," replies Walmsley.

"Thank you for your honesty, Mayor Walmsley," says Nathan.

"Mayor Walmsley, if there's anything else that you need from us, let me know. We're ready to get going now," says Alonzo. Walmsley stands and walks to his office door. He opens the door for Ora and Louise. Ora follows Louise out to the lobby and Alonzo and Nathan join them.

"That was horrible," says Nathan.

"I'm very sorry, Nathan. The meeting was disappointing. Let's get out of here," Alonzo says. He takes Louise's hand and walks toward Camp Street with Nathan and Ora.

"Now do you understand why I never wanted you to confront Walmsley?" asks Nathan.

"Yes, Papa. He's terrible. I don't want to have anything to do with Walmsley ever again," says Ora.

"I thought that Walmsley was going to reach over his desk and strike Alonzo for a moment there," says Louise.

"I would have hit him first," says Alonzo.

"City Hall is in hell with Walmsley in office. Can New Orleans ever escape his grip?" asks Nathan.

"We can fight him and win. We just have to be very careful from now on. He's warned us, so we won't have a second chance," says Alonzo. They reach the car and he opens the doors for everyone as they climb in. Alonzo turns the ignition on and drives toward Poydras Street.

"Nathan and Ora, thank you so much for being there today. I know that the meeting was a disaster, but it could have been much worse for me without you there," Alonzo says.

"It was worth it to finally hear Walmsley admit that he's a white supremacist. He's just a liar. He'll never regain credibility," Nathan says.

"I assumed that Walmsley would pretend and engage with us the way that he always does with the press. He didn't hide very much about his aggression with us today," Ora says.

"Ora, Walmsley is an extremist. He went from being extremely powerful to being extremely desperate in less than a year. He's definitely on his way out," says Louise.

"I can't believe that he ordered us to stop all coverage of his administration today. I guess that it's his last hope to rebuild," Alonzo says.

"His yelling was so distasteful. He's a racist coward with a terrible attitude. He should have never been elected mayor," Nathan says.

"If he requests another meeting, I'll just decline and hope for the best," Alonzo says. He turns onto Broad

Avenue from Poydras Street.

"I knew that Walmsley was horrible, but I guess I hoped for something a little different from him today," says Ora.

"That was mild compared to what he's done in our community. He could have hurt us very badly today. Maybe he's afraid to reveal himself to us," Alonzo says.

"Walmsley's not afraid. He's buying time and trying to change his image. Hurting us will only make him look like the monster that he is," Nathan says.

"Let's begin to think about our new approach to desegregation now that we've been banned from covering Walmsley," Louise says.

"There's not much we can do until he resigns, Louise. The good thing is that the story is part of the daily news in the city now," Alonzo says.

"I think I've had just about enough of New Orleans. I'm ready to get back to Baton Rouge and distance myself from Walmsley," says Nathan. Alonzo turns onto Washington Avenue from Broad Avenue.

"Nathan, you'll be back before you know it. The charm of the city will lure you in despite the disappointments," says Alonzo.

"I know that the city will be restored. Imagine if Robert Maestri became mayor. We would all be so happy," Ora says.

"You're right. We just have to work hard and support Robert's possible campaign. We can meet with him and let him know all about what happened today at City Hall," says Alonzo.

"Robert will be surprised to hear that Walmsley actually met with us today. He's going to be upset about Walmsley's blackout demands, but he'll be relieved that he didn't take it any further," Nathan says.

"Robert has done so well in the news since the *Times Picayune* covered the protest. When he announced his intentions to run for mayor in the paper, so many people in the city were encouraged," Ora says.

"Robert really has turned out to be a savvy leader. He's already outmaneuvered Walmsley," says Nathan.

"Robert can pick up where we left off, providing the press with the information needed to bury Walmsley in damaging stories," says Louise.

"Robert has already begun reaching out to the Old Regulars for their support. Once they've selected him as Walmsley's successor, it's a done deal," explains Alonzo.

"I'm so glad that I'm able to be a part of Robert's success story. When he's mayor, we'll never be attacked again in City Hall," Ora says.

"I'll definitely be back when that happens," says Nathan. Alonzo pulls into the driveway at his office. He parks his car and opens the doors for Louise and Ora.

"Well, Nathan, I know this wasn't anything like our meetings with Huey P. Long, but we survived the day," Alonzo says.

Nathan shakes Alonzo's hand. "You're a fighter and I respect that about you. Let's keep our eyes on the future and do everything we can to get rid of Walmsley," says Nathan.

"I hope to see you again soon," says Alonzo.

"I don't know when I'll be back, but I'll come to check on Ora before too long," Nathan says.

"I'll see you bright and early tomorrow morning, Alonzo and Louise," says Ora.

"Try to enjoy what's left of the day," Alonzo replies. Ora and Nathan walk to his car and he opens the door for Ora. She climbs into the car and Nathan walks around to the driver's side and enters.

Nathan drives toward Washington Avenue from

Erato Street. "Ora, you probably already know how I feel about you being here," he says.

"Papa, I can't just leave New Orleans and Alonzo behind, because of a hostile warning from Walmsley. I have my entire career in front of me here," Ora says.

"You can start over in Baton Rouge and do well. You can finish school and study at Southern," Nathan says.

"Papa, it's just not the same. So many people in the city depend on me for honest in-depth coverage of segregation. I can't just let them all down," Ora says.

"Ora, you're going to soon realize that people appreciate your efforts no matter what. You're not obligated to stay here when your life is in danger," explains Nathan.

"Walmsley said all that he needed to say to us today. The fight is over. I accept that and I'm ready to move on," says Ora.

"Ora, Alonzo will not stop fighting with Walmsley. You're in the line of fire with him. Just be careful from now on," says Nathan. He turns onto Claiborne Avenue toward Annette Street.

"Today changed my understanding of Walmsley's hatred. I will not risk my life to cover him ever again," says Ora.

"Now that's what I want to hear from my brilliant baby girl," Nathan says.

"Papa, I'm sorry for ever doubting you. I'm not sorry for organizing the protest, but I know now that I've risked it all along the way," says Ora.

"Ora, you're going to be just fine. Remember your commitment to avoid Walmsley until this whole thing is over and you'll never have to look back to days like today," Nathan says.

"Papa, I want to remember today. I want to celebrate our new mayor and think back to the struggle and the fight, appreciating the ultimate victory," says Ora.

"Ora, when you have a daughter who's as feisty as you are, you'll understand how difficult it is to protect her," Nathan says. Ora laughs.

"What would you do without my intrigue in your life, Papa?" asks Ora. Nathan smiles.

"I would be happy, but I would be bored stiff," he says. They both laugh together. Nathan pulls up to the curb of Ora's house and walks around to the passenger side to open the door for her.

Ora hugs her father and says, "Goodbye for now, Papa."

"Remember to call me each day. You know how worried I am about you right now," Nathan says.

"It's almost over. Please pray for us here in New Orleans," Ora says.

"You know I'm praying for you, Ora. Your spirit keeps me alive," Nathan says. Nathan climbs into his car and waves goodbye to Ora. She walks to the front door and enters the house.

"Ora, you made it back early," Josephine says.

"The meeting was brief. Walmsley had a lot to say, but he said it loudly and quickly," Ora says.

"We've been in prayer for you, Ora. We just didn't know what to expect," says Josephine.

"Ora, come in and have a seat. You must be exhausted," Ellis says.

"We've prepared lunch for you and we can't wait to hear about the meeting," Josephine says. Ora enters the kitchen and takes a seat at the table.

"Ma Mere and Ma Mum, Mayor Walmsley was terrible. He kicked and screamed all morning. He's forbidden us from ever writing about him again," explains Ora.

"Well good riddance. You have serious work to do

to turn the city around. We're just counting down the days until he finally leaves," Josephine says.

"It's not fair that he would threaten you that way. What did Alonzo have to say about it?" Ellis asks.

"Alonzo was surprisingly calm. He apologized to Papa for the meeting," replies Ora.

"Alonzo is not going to take this lying down. He's going to put an end to Walmsley's administration somehow," says Josephine.

"Ma Mere, I don't know. Alonzo is very discouraged this time. He seems to have a plan, but Walmsley really affected him today," says Ora.

"Alonzo always has a plan. Just believe in his methods and follow his guidance. He's a difference maker," says Josephine.

"Ora, I prepared fried trout, okra and potatoes for you. Are you hungry?" asks Ellis.

"You know it. All of the fussing and fighting has built my appetite," replies Ora. Josephine places the meal on the table for them. Ellis and Josephine have a seat next to Ora.

"Heavenly Father, bless this meal, bless our family and our home. Thank you for this day, God. Amen," says

Josephine.

Ora begins to enjoy the meal. "The trout and okra are delicious. Thank you so much, Ma Mum," says Ora.

"You're welcome, Ora. I'm glad to cook for you, honey," says Ellis.

"So, Ora, what did Walmsley really say today?" inquires Josephine.

"Ma Mere, Walmsley lied from the moment we walked through the door. He denied any involvement in the murders, shootings and arrests," Ora replies.

"Of course he did, Ora. He's a murderer," Josephine says.

"He did admit one thing," Ora says.

"What's that?" asks Ellis.

"He said that he is a white supremacist and that he avoids involvement in the attacks of Black people," Ora explains.

"Really?!" asks Josephine.

"That's very surprising, considering his clean-cut image," Ellis says.

"Alonzo pretty much walked out on the meeting after Walmsley's admission. He was so disappointed by his tone and his approach," says Ora.

"Alonzo is so dignified. He could have really given Walmsley a piece of his mind, but he just let Walmsley have his way, didn't he?" asks Josephine.

"That's right. He asked Walmsley a few questions, but he complied with his demands," Ora replies.

"Well, Ora, you've now seen the worst of it all in the city. It's very much a part of life as a Black person in this day and age. The difference is that you're doing something about it. I'm so proud of you," Josephine says.

"It could be worse, Ma Mere. Just imagine how wonderful it will be when Robert Maestri becomes mayor. We'll live so well," Ora says.

"It will be better, but segregation will still remain. We can't stop fighting even after Maestri has won," says Josephine.

"Just remember this day and how discouraged we feel. Our pain and suffering will be a distant memory when segregation finally comes to an end," Ora says.

CHAPTER 9 / "THE TRANSFORMATION"

Excited city workers rush to prepare for the major ceremony of the historic day. American flags and banners cover the mounted gallery of City Hall. Thousands of people are gathered to witness one of the most anticipated events of the decade. Black children leap for joy as the festivities begin. Although the massive crowd is racially divided, the people celebrate harmoniously. The sweet smell of candy and treats fills the summer air. The sun shines brightly in the beautifully clear sky.

A white dove flies down to Ora's feet and she is

reminded of her mother Cecilia. Miraculously, the dove is transformed into an image of Ora's mother. Ora reaches out to touch her mother and her hand is covered by a gentle spirit. Cecilia's face and hair glisten brightly. She is robed in an angelic white gown. Ora sees her mother's face for the first time in eleven years. She is overjoyed to be in the presence of her mother's spirit. As she experiences this heavenly moment, Ora realizes that she has reached a spiritual precipice. All of the hurt and the pain suffered by the people as Mayor Walmsley controlled the tattered city has begun to heal.

When Mayor Walmsley was finally forced to resign, the people were elated. He relinquished his reign of terror and abuse in exchange for a legislative overhaul of Huey P. Long's laws that stripped him of his financial power. The continuous press coverage of Walmsley's murders and attacks of Black people annihilated his image. Walmsley lost what remained of his support from the Old Regulars and the conservative right. He could no longer convince the people that he was reasonable and fair. His extreme hatred could no longer be hidden. Ora, Alonzo and Nathan were silenced, but their influence was overwhelming. There was nothing that Walmsley could do to repair the shattered perception of his administration.

Within eight days of his meeting with Ora, Alonzo, Nathan and Louise, Walmsley announced his resignation. He survived opposition and accusations from Huey P. Long, but he could not sustain power after Ora's protest. While Long accused Walmsley of plotting to assassinate him, the press now tied Walmsley to brutal murders and attacks that couldn't be denied. Walmsley ordered members of the White League to hunt down Black people who openly opposed him. He had them beaten, arrested and murdered. Some of the victims were former city employees, while others were vocal political organizers. Walmsley attempted to hide the stories of their murders from the press by having the police accuse them of crimes and characterizing them as criminals. He created a political underworld that haunted the Black community in New Orleans.

Mayor Walmsley was notorious for his white supremacist beliefs, but he was able to mask his hatred. By day, Walmsley cajoled the press. By night, he roamed the streets of the Black community in search of dissidents. Walmsley led his own small apartheid in a city isolated from the liberal supporters who were unaware of the suffering. President Roosevelt hoped for a change in administration, but he worked from a distance. When the press finally exposed Walmsley's violence, the president was relieved to see that efforts had been made to release his grip on the weakening city. Although many of the people supported Huey P. Long, President Roosevelt embraced them as his own. He knew that without Senator Long and Governor Oscar K. Allen, Louisiana would be at the mercy of white supremacists. Ora looked to President Roosevelt for words of wisdom as she fought to free the city from Walmsley's violence. She hoped for his involvement, but she did not wait for his approval. Ora knew that President Roosevelt would be glad to see Walmsley finally leave and she expected his support for the resignation.

As Ora watches the image of her mother, she finally feels at peace with the conditions of her life. Ora's experience with the death of Huey P. Long encouraged her to appreciate the years that she was able to spend with her mother as a child. Ora often felt so alone without her mother. She felt that she missed out on experiences that could have changed her world and her outlook on life. Yet, she understood that her sense of responsibility as the eldest child honed her instincts and transformed her into a genuine leader. Ora was so discouraged by Walmsley's murders and violence. Her coverage of the attacks was cryptic and melancholy, but the people appreciated her honesty.

Ora's connection with her mother was meaningful and powerful. Cecilia was an exceptional pianist, yet Ora also remembers her parents discussing segregation openly. Cecilia was adamant about equality in education and Nathan often described segregation in the military during the First World War. Ora overheard Nathan discussing a lynching and Cecilia urging him to be careful when traveling. Her parents were once inseparable. They loved each other very much and their love for Ora was unmistakable. As a child, Ora was taught that she could do anything that she worked hard to accomplish. Her mother nourished her love for reading as well as writing at a very early age. Cecilia recognized Ora's gifts and she invested a great deal in her success.

When Cecilia's health deteriorated, her greatest concern was her children and their future. She lost the fight for her life when her doctors failed to find a remedy for her condition. Ora was devastated to lose her mother. She cherished each moment spent with Cecilia. Ora prayed for her mother's recovery and she could not understand how Cecilia could suffer so severely in such a short period of time. Ora's suffering would last a lifetime and she was heartbroken by the loss. Her pain was genuine and she was truly able to identify with victims of Mayor Walmsley's violence. Ora did receive an inheritance of faith from her mother that was enduring. She remembered attending church with her mother and their time of prayer together. Ora honored her mother's faith by dedicating her life to God and to service. As Ora looks at Cecilia's face, she watches her image vanish and transform into the white dove. She smiles and thanks God for the spiritual blessing. Ora turns to Nathan and says, "Papa, God is present with us today. He revealed Mama to me. I am so blessed."

"You will see her again. She's here, because you have helped to transform New Orleans, Ora," Nathan says. "Let's join your grandmothers, Cleo and Alexia in the gallery ahead."

"Today is the big day. Robert Maestri has finally been elected mayor unopposed," Ora says. Nathan leads her toward the section for Robert's special guests. Ora is wearing a formal white dress and Nathan is wearing an English cut black suit. City officials are dressed in formal attire for the momentous occasion. Ora and Nathan see Alonzo and Louise up ahead speaking with Governor Richard Leche and Lieutenant Governor Earl K. Long.

"Ora, your victory means so much to the people of the city," Josephine says.

"You've touched the lives of so many people, Ora," says Ellis.

"Having you here to celebrate with me is a miracle. You mean the world to me," Ora says.

"Ora, I would like to introduce Governor Leche and Lieutenant Governor Long to you," Nathan says.

"Ma Mere and Ma Mum, I will soon return," Ora says as she follows her father. The two of them approach Earl and Richard.

"Lieutenant Governor Long, you may be familiar with our young writer, Ora Lewis," Alonzo says.

"It's a pleasure to finally meet after hearing about you from Huey. Congratulations, Ora," says Earl.

"Thank you, Lieutenant Governor Long. We couldn't have done it without you," says Ora.

"Nathan, you must be very proud of your talented daughter," Earl says.

"Ora was born with a gift. The challenge is to

protect her from the many dangers that she fights as a journalist," says Nathan.

"Alonzo has provided Ora with the support needed to transform the city. Your protection is vital to maintain her momentum," Earl says.

"Walmsley was a top priority for my office. The work that you have done is invaluable," Richard says.

"I'm honored to meet you, Governor Leche and Lieutenant Governor Long. My father speaks very highly of you," Ora says.

"Ora, we're human just like you. We have fears and weaknesses too. When we meet young people with your courage, we're very encouraged about the future," Earl says.

"I never realized that you were there supporting our efforts to bring an end to the Walmsley administration. I was so focused on planning and organizing, that I didn't look to you for answers," Ora says.

"That's why we're so proud of you, Ora. You really made a difference for the people," Earl says.

"When Huey P. Long passed away, I decided to become the leader we lost and needed," Ora says.

"That's what makes you so special, Ora," Earl says.

"We're prepared for the next chapter in the history of New Orleans. Our worst days are behind us," Alonzo says.

"New Orleans won't be healed until Jim Crow segregation has come to an end," Earl says.

"Jim Crow is only as bad as the leaders who enforce it," Nathan says.

"We will do all that we can to fight segregation and support the leaders who believe in freedom," says Earl.

"That means a great deal to us, Lieutenant Governor Long," says Nathan.

"Our expectations are high for Robert Maestri. We're confident that he will restore the city," Richard says.

"We worked with Robert to plan his campaign. He attended our protest and spoke to the people," Alonzo says.

"His track record is solid. He can bring much needed change to the city," says Richard.

"Robert planned his campaign perfectly. He made the right impression on the press and overshadowed Walmsley completely," Alonzo says.

"That's good politics," says Richard.

"Today's inauguration is just the beginning for us. I'd like you all to work closely with our office from today forward," Earl says.

"That would be wonderful, Lieutenant Governor Long. Although Huey P. Long is no longer with us, we can honor his memory by working with you to restore the city," Ora says.

"That's what Huey would have wanted. I wish that he could be here with us today," Earl says.

"He's here in spirit. None of this would be possible without him," Nathan says.

"Lieutenant Governor Long, do you still think about how it would have been if Huey P. Long had been elected president?" asks Ora.

"I think about it every day. He would have been an excellent president. They'll never be another Huey," replies Earl.

"I didn't realize that he was so dynamic until I finally had a chance to meet him. He changed America forever," says Ora.

"What you may not have known about Huey was that he took major risks. He would have been much more aggressive than Robert Maestri in a run for mayor. He would have publicly challenged Walmsley in the press and demanded his resignation," says Earl.

"You're right about that," laughs Alonzo. "Huey was relentless."

"Huey P. Long was Walmsley's strongest opponent. Walmsley unleashed his most violent attacks after his passing. We were defenseless against Walmsley for a time," Nathan says.

"We're just so relieved that Walmsley is finally gone. Your efforts proved to be most effective," Earl says.

The band plays "King Cotton March" as the inauguration begins. The crowd roars with applause as Robert Maestri enters the gallery. City officials give the mayor-elect a standing ovation. Ora, Nathan, Alonzo and Louise rush down to their seats next to Josephine and Ellis waving goodbye to Earl and Richard.

Reverend Carl Dixon approaches the podium to deliver the benediction. "Today we celebrate a new beginning for the great City of New Orleans. We celebrate Robert Maestri as our new mayor and leader. Not only does he represent a renewed sense of hope, but he will bring peace to a city torn apart by violence and divisiveness. Though we have been affected by hatred, we have not been destroyed. We can rebuild through faith and a commitment to God. May God bless the hands and heart of Robert

Maestri, inspiring him to lead us all in a new way. We thank you, God for this day and we praise you for the blessing of hope." Everyone applauds Reverend Dixon's words.

Governor Richard Leche approaches the podium to deliver his address. "The City of New Orleans is one of the most important historic sites in America. We could not afford to lose its heritage and its people any longer. The day that Robert Maestri declared his intentions to run for mayor was a momentous occasion for the state. We are so proud of Robert Maestri and we are proud of the City of New Orleans. Remember this day and this occasion. Consider the great efforts made to make this day possible. Remember the lives that were lost as we waited for the election of our new mayor. We deserve brighter days and they have finally arrived for each one of us, no matter what our station in life may be. Dignity has been restored to the office of mayor of the City of New Orleans." The crowd applauds for Governor Leche.

Associate Justice Archie T. Higgins approaches the podium to deliver the oath of office. Robert Maestri follows him and stands at the podium raising his right hand. "Do you, Robert Sidney Maestri solemnly swear that you will support the Constitution of the United States, and the Louisiana Constitution, and the Charter of the City of New Orleans?" asks Archie.

"I do," replies Robert.

"Do you swear that you will faithfully discharge the duties of the office of the Mayor of the City of New Orleans to the best of your ability?" asks Archie.

"I do. So, help me God," replies Robert.

"Congratulations, Mayor Robert Maestri," says Archie as he shakes Robert's hand. Everyone cheers in excitement for their new mayor.

Robert waves to the crowd and claps for them as well. He takes the podium and begins his inaugural address. "I am truly honored to be the new mayor of the City of New Orleans. Your support for me has been overwhelming. When I began my political career as a member of the Huey P. Long administration, I never imagined that I would one day lead the city that I had called home throughout my life. I love this city and I have a vision for its revival that is not limited by the race or status of its people. I made the decision to run for mayor when I realized that the quality of life in the city had been devalued by violence and hatred that could destroy us all. My wealth and influence was not enough to right the blatant wrongs. I knew that I needed to become the new mayor. I faced dangers from leaders who had a habit of attacking opponents, but I was not afraid to stand in the face of adversity.

I have a small group of brave journalists to thank for your support. They reminded me that there is power in numbers and that faith can move mountains. It is a privilege to work with the journalists as they prepare our community for change that may seem impossible in this day and age. I am grateful to them and I will continue to support their peaceful efforts as mayor," Robert states. Ora, Nathan and Alonzo smile as they receive recognition for their efforts.

"I would like to thank Governor Richard Leche and Lieutenant Governor Earl K. Long for their support of our people and our major plans for the city. Their work with the Louisiana Legislature will free the city from the many restrictions that have cost us our financial viability. This road will not be easy, but it will lead us to a promising future. I owe it all to the people of New Orleans and I thank you for your trust is me as your new mayor," Robert proclaims. The crowd erupts with applause for Robert as he shakes Earl's hand. Robert's parents embrace him and congratulate him. Robert finds Ora, Alonzo and Nathan in the crowd and waves at them in appreciation. They wave at Robert and clap for him. A marching band approaches Gallier Hall on Saint Charles Avenue performing "Chimes of Liberty." The people are so excited to welcome their new mayor to City Hall. The mood is celebratory and joyous.

"He's finally mayor of New Orleans. What a miracle," Alonzo exclaims.

"He thanked us in his address. That was a powerful moment," Ora notes.

"You have a mayor who cares a great deal about the people. He truly appreciates the support that you've given to him," Nathan adds.

"This day will always be remembered as the day that the City of New Orleans was reborn. My work has just begun to bring desegregation to the people who have placed their trust in me. I will not stop until my life's work is done," declares Ora.